Haunted by the ghosts of her grandfather and his war-time bomber crew, Meg tries to make sense of the warnings they give. The development of a neglected piece of land into a conservation area adds to her supernatural experiences, which disturb her sleep and her school work. What is the message – and will Meg be able to convince those around her of its importance?

'This well-plotted book . . . proceeds to a genuinely exciting climax.'
Junior Bookshelf

'. . . pleasantly easy read.'
The Times Educational Supplement

About the author

Robert Swindells has lived in the
Bradford area throughout his life.

After a wide variety of work – as
copyholder, airman, primary school
teacher – he now writes full-time and has
written some twenty books for children.

Married with two daughters, he is an
active member of the Peace Movement.

The Ghost
Messengers

Robert Swindells

KNIGHT BOOKS
Hodder and Stoughton

First published in Great Britain in 1986 by Hodder and Stoughton Children's Books

New edition 1988

This impression 1990

British Library C.I.P.

Swindells, Robert, *1939–*
    The ghost messengers.
    I. Title
    823'.914[J]

ISBN 0 340 48668 6

Printed and bound in Great Britain for Hodder and Stoughton Paperbacks, a division of Hodder and Stoughton Ltd., Mill Road, Dunton Green, Sevenoaks, Kent TN13 2YA. (Editorial Office: 47 Bedford Square, London WC1B 3DP) by Cox & Wyman Ltd., Reading.

One

Meg came awake and opened her eyes and he was there again – a silhouette against the curtain. She couldn't see his face but she knew it was him. He had appeared from time to time like this ever since she could remember: watching her with his sad eyes. He never spoke. One or twice she'd whispered, 'Grandad?' but he hadn't answered her. Perhaps he couldn't. Ghosts in stories shriek and moan, but that's in stories. Perhaps when you're dead you have no voice.

She lay still, gazing at him across the dim room. She was not afraid. When he began to fade she smiled. She liked to think it made him happy to see her smile, but since he never spoke there was no way of knowing.

When he'd gone she lay staring up into the dark. Where did he go, she wondered, when he left her? Did he go to wherever it was his bones lay? Was he unhappy because nobody knew where they were? Might he have rested better if they'd found his bomber and buried him properly?

The darkness above her seemed full of moving things and her eyelids grew heavy, and yet she didn't sleep. She couldn't, because a part of her had followed the phantom and was out there somewhere, wandering. Those of us who sleep soundly are more fortunate than we know, for it is a fact that two sorts of spirits haunt the night: those of the restless dead, and the spirits of those who live, and know no rest.

Two

She didn't mention the ghost at breakfast. There was no point. She'd tried telling them once when she was smaller, but they'd laughed and said she'd dreamt it. She had insisted tearfully that she'd been wide awake, and that he was exactly like the snapshot on the sideboard. Her mother had grown suddenly angry then and snapped at her, saying that it wasn't nice to make up stories about people who had died and so, though she had seen him many times in her room, and once or twice outside in broad daylight, she'd never spoken of it again.

Now breakfast was almost over. Mum sipped her coffee. Paul was pushing a bit of bacon around his plate and Dad had retreated behind the paper. The Ravens were not really morning people, and breakfast was always a subdued affair. Meg had learned early in life that it was wise to keep a low profile at breakfast.

The silence was broken now by Dad, who rattled the paper and looked at his family over the top of it.

'How d'you fancy a nature park and leisure reserve on the doorstep?' he asked. Mrs Raven put down her cup.

'A what, dear?'

'A nature park and leisure reserve,' her husband repeated. 'It says here that the Council's thinking of turning Judy Woods into a nature park and leisure reserve as an amenity for the people of the area.'

Paul snorted. He was seventeen and cynical about everything.

'It's already an amenity for the people of the area,' he growled. 'Everybody dumps their rubbish there, it's a snogging-place for couples in cars and a scramble-track for every bike-boy in York.'

'I know,' his father replied, 'but it says here that they'll get kids on a training scheme to clean the place up. You might even find yourself doing it, old lad. And when it's done there'll be a warden to keep an eye on it. There'll be lavatories and an eating place and a car park. It sounds like a good idea to me.'

'It'll bring everybody out from the city,' said Paul. 'It'll be like Piccadilly Circus on a fine weekend.'

'That may not be a bad thing,' his mother told him. 'It would mean extra business for the village shops and goodness knows they can do with it.'

'Yes,' added Meg. 'And the warden would keep the bikes away and see that nobody dumped old mattresses and stuff there any more. It's work for some of the people who have none and like Dad says, one of them could be you, Paul.'

Paul snorted again. 'Some work,' he sneered. 'How would you like to get six O-levels and then find yourself picking up trash in Judy Woods? What's that got to do with training for God's sake?'

'Paul!' His mother frowned at him. 'Mind your language, please. Cleaning up the environment may not be something you'd choose to do, but it is worthwhile and it's certainly better than doing nothing.'

'No it's not!' Paul pushed back his chair and stood up. 'I'd rather do nothing any day than go round touching smelly mattresses that someone's died on and crummy old . . .'

'That'll do, lad!' Mr Raven glared at his son. 'At least you've got a place on a scheme. Thousands haven't. And we don't particularly want to listen to your opinions at the breakfast table. Go and get ready, or you'll be sacked and end up hanging about the streets all day.'

The boy left the room muttering. Mrs Raven got up and began clearing the table and her husband went to get the car out. Meg sat on for a while, thinking. Wilberforce was a boring place to live in most of the time. A nature park and leisure reserve might liven the place up a bit. She smiled. It had certainly livened up breakfast this morning, and anything that did that in this house couldn't be bad.

Three

At ten past eight Dad left with Paul in the car. Paul's training centre was in York and Dad dropped him off each morning. Dad was Advertisement Manager with an evening paper called the Star. Meg reckoned he took Paul to make sure he actually went to the centre.

When they had gone, Meg wiped the breakfast things and packed her bag. She was twelve, and went to Wilberforce Junior and Infant School. It wasn't a bad place, but she could hardly wait to be thirteen and go to Paul's old school in the city. Not because it was Paul's old school, though – Paul was a pain, and the older he got the worse he seemed to become. He'd been okay once, when Meg was small and they both went to Wilberforce J. and I. He'd never actually played with her, but he'd stuck up for her against the bigger kids till she learned to fend for herself. No: she wanted to go to the upper school because they treated you like a grown-up there and she'd ride in with Dad each morning. Paul's training would be over by then. He might even have left home, with a bit of luck.

She sighed, put on her cardigan and hung the bag on her shoulder. Her mother was upstairs making beds. 'I'm off now, Mum!' she called.

'All right, dear. Give Grandma my love, and come straight home this afternoon.'

Meg's lips formed the words as her mother spoke them. She'd heard them five mornings a week for more than a year. She called, 'Yes, Mum,' in a bored voice. ' 'Bye!'

Mum was writing a book. A novel. She'd been at it for a year and it wasn't anywhere near finished yet. Meg thought that if it ever got printed it would be about two feet thick. Because of this book, Meg went to her Grandma's for lunch

8

every weekday. That gave Mum time to get through the housework and put in a couple of hours writing before starting the evening meal. Grandma was typing the novel, too, bit by bit as Mum wrote it. She used to be a secretary before she retired.

It was April, and the sun glowed behind a veil of mist as Meg walked down Newside Avenue and turned left along the High Street. Children in groups straggled towards the school, chattering. Others sped by on bicycles, calling and ringing their bells. Here and there were mothers with pushchairs and infants in tow.

Sally was waiting at the end of Newside Road as usual. She was Meg's best friend. It was only a hundred yards from Newside Road to the school gate, but the two girls always walked it together. It was nice to have a bit of a chat before lessons got in the way. Today they talked about the plan for Judy Woods, which lay just beyond the school playing-field.

'I think it's a super idea,' said Sally. 'Our mums will let us play there, instead of telling us to keep away because of the motor-bikes and the rubbish.'

Meg nodded, grinning. 'I know. And on Saturdays we'll be able to go and sit in the cafe and have coke and ice-cream and there might be a juke-box with good records in it.'

At lunchtime, Meg crossed the High Street and hurried towards her grandma's house. This side of the street was where the old part of the village lay. Fox Place, where Grandma lived, was almost opposite her own home in Newside Avenue. It was named after the inn on the Green – the Fox. Meg hoped her grandad would be having his lunch at the Fox today, as he often did when he was working on his allotment. Her step-grandad, as Mum always called him. The man Grandma married after her husband disappeared in the war. It wasn't that Meg didn't like him. He was the only grandad she had ever known and he had always been very kind to her, but she knew Mum didn't care for him much, and she'd always felt it was disloyal to show him affection. She even felt guilty when she called him Grandad.

He was out. Grandma had made a shepherd's pie for lunch. They sat, the two of them, eating and chatting.

'How's your Mum today?'

'Oh, she's okay. She sends her love as usual. Is Grandad all right?' There it was again; that little twinge of guilt. Her grandmother nodded.

'He's fine dear, thank you. Busy with the allotment and lunching with his cronies at the Fox. He's a bit stirred up over this Judy Woods affair though. Nearly had a fit when he read this morning's paper.'

'Why?' Meg was astonished. 'It seems like a really super idea to me and everybody else thinks so too. Except Paul of course – he thinks nobody ever has good ideas except him.'

Her grandmother chuckled. 'Ah, well you see – your grandad was a farmer all his life till he retired, and farmers don't reckon much to town people. He's afraid this nature park thing will bring folk flocking out here from York, breaking down walls and leaving gates open. Some of his friends will feel the same way, I fancy – it wouldn't surprise me if they're hatching some sort of plot in the Fox at this moment – a protest group or something of that sort.'

'Really?' Meg's eyes widened. 'That'd be terrific, Grandma. Wilberforce is such a boring place. It'll be great if people start having marches and sit-ins all over the place. We'll get in the papers and everything. Oh, I hope you're right – I hope they are forming a protest group. Even though I think they're wrong,' she added.

'Well I hope they're doing nothing of the kind,' said her grandmother, firmly. 'I don't see why people can't get along together in a friendly way. There's far too much protesting and marching and agitating in the world if you ask me. It always ends in tears. Somebody goes a bit too far and starts a fight and then people get hurt.' She got up and started to clear the table.

Meg dabbed her lips with her napkin to hide the smile that had broken out, but it showed in her eyes. She rose to help, carrying the cruet set to the cupboard. Her grandmother turned on the hot tap and squirted washing-up liquid into the sink.

'I can see you think it's funny, my girl,' she said. 'But believe me there's nothing funny about fighting. The trouble is, it's not the people who start the fighting who get hurt. It's other people: people who only wanted to be left alone to get on with their lives. People like your first grandad – your real one.'

Meg heard the break in the old lady's voice and when she looked there were tears in her eyes. She dabbed at them with a tissue and blew her nose.

'Oh, yes,' she sniffed. 'Grown-ups cry too you see. It's embarrassing isn't it? I remember once as a child, I was at a funeral. I've forgotten whose funeral it was but suddenly there were all those adults, sniffling and wiping their eyes. It looked ridiculous to me.' She crushed the tissue and dropped it in the pedal-bin, smiling tightly.

'Don't look at me like that, dear – I'm all right now. It's just that it always seems such a terrible waste. I mean, we're all the best of friends now, aren't we? Us and the Germans. So why did we have to fall out in the first place? Why did we have to slaughter so many of each other's young men?'

Meg felt a rush of pity for her. She wanted to say, 'I see him, Grandma: he comes to me,' but of course she couldn't. The old lady wouldn't believe her – would think she was playing a cruel game. She picked up the tea-towel and began to dry the dishes as her grandmother slotted them into the rack.

When it was time to go she said, 'I didn't mean fighting, Grandma – of course I wouldn't want that. I only meant excitement, that's all. A bit of excitement.'

'I know dear.' Her grandmother gave her a brief hug. 'I'm becoming a silly old woman and you're not to take any notice of me.'

But in spite of the hug, Meg felt confused and unhappy as she walked back to school.

Four

At four o'clock Sally said, 'Let's go and see if anything's happening in the woods yet.'

Meg shook her head. 'Can't. Mum made me promise to come straight home. Anyway, nothing'll be happening yet. They've only just had the idea.'

'It wouldn't take long,' Sally persuaded, 'and you never know. They might be surveying or something. Come on, Meg.'

Meg slung her bag on her shoulder and waited as Sally tied her shoelaces. Her friend was right, of course. The woods were nearby and it wouldn't take a minute to go and have a look. Not that Meg thought they'd see anything but as Sally said, you never know.

'All right,' she said. 'But only for a minute, Sal. I'm not going to hang about and get played heck with by my mum.'

Sally tugged her lace tight and straightened up. 'Okay,' she grinned. 'Let's go.'

They skirted the school building, slanted across the playing-field and shinned over the fence. There was a scrubby bit of pasture with a goat tethered on it, and then the woods. In less than a minute they were standing under the first trees. A couple of boys passed them, taking a short-cut home. Otherwise the woods seemed quiet.

'It's too soon, Sal,' said Meg. 'I told you it would be.'

Her friend shrugged. 'We haven't really looked, have we? I mean, we might as well go in a bit now that we're here.'

She began walking into the wood. Meg glanced at her watch, pulled a face and followed.

The sun was low in the sky and the light grew dim as they threaded their way between close-growing trunks of oak and sycamore. They scrunched over a carpet of last year's leaves, through which bluebell and bracken were thrusting their pale fresh spikes and curls. After a while they came to the wide pathway which bisected the wood, and Meg stopped.

'Hang on, Sal,' she said. 'This is where people would be if there were any, but there aren't. I'm off home.'

Sally stopped reluctantly, and stood looking at the ground, kicking bits of twig about. 'Boggy Hollow's just round the bend,' she said. 'You can leave me if you want to, but I'm going to have a look. I'll see you.' She turned and began to walk away.

Meg called after her, 'Wait!' She didn't want to go back alone. Parents and teachers were always warning them never to be alone in the woods. There were supposed to be funny people about, whatever that meant, and whatever it meant it scared her to death.

Sally turned and Meg said, 'You promised we'd only be a minute. It's dangerous by yourself. Come on home.'

Sally shook her head. There was a stubborn streak in her. 'No. You go if you like. I'm not scared. I'll see you tomorrow.'

'You might not,' Meg retorted. 'You might be found strangled like that girl in Fitzroy Park. She wasn't scared, either.'

It was no use. Sally turned and walked on. Meg stood watching her for a moment then hurried after her, muttering to herself.

Boggy Hollow was a bowl-shaped, marshy depression in the middle of the wood. Out of its black, evil-smelling waters rose a dense tangle of alder and hazel, growing so thickly that it would have been virtually impossible to force a way through them, in the unlikely event of anybody wanting to. In summer it was infested with clouds of gnats and midges and in winter it was a black, brooding place, suggestive of trolls and boggarts. The pathway skirted Boggy Hollow in a broad curve and, though many people gazed down into it as they passed by, few bothered to go closer.

The two girls stood at the edge of the path, looking down. The banking here was strewn with debris and churned to mud by motor cycle wheels. Boggy Hollow itself was at its best – its winter blackness softened by a yellow-green haze of buds and catkins. At the foot of the slope a rusty pram lay on its side in one of the sluggish streams which emptied themselves into the marsh.

'There, you see?' Meg's tone was smug. 'Nothing, just like I said. Can we go home now?'

Sally shrugged. 'I suppose so,' she muttered. 'But there might have been something – I'm glad we checked.' She turned and began walking back along the path. Meg was about to follow when her eyes were drawn to some slight movement, down where the alders began. The sun had gone behind the trees and the light was difficult, but when she looked carefully she saw that a man was standing in the shadow, watching them.

'Sal!' At Meg's hiss, her friend turned and Meg motioned her to come back. Sally came, frowning.

'What's up?' she demanded. 'I thought you said . . .'

'Look.' Meg drew her close and pointed. 'There's a man down there, watching us.' Her heart was thumping and she held herself poised to run. 'It might be one of those funny people they go on about at school.'

Her friend scanned the place through screwed-up eyes and said, 'Is there heck!'

'Yes there is – look.' Meg grabbed her arm and pointed again. 'See that fallen tree? Well, just to the left of it and a bit further in – see?'

Sally looked and shook her head. 'There's nobody there, Meg. Just shadows. Look – I'll prove it to you.'

Before Meg could stop her, Sally went bounding down the treacherous slope, her arms flung out for balance.

'No – come back, Sal!' Meg stood wild-eyed on the brink. Down there lurked the very danger they'd been warned of so often, for what ordinary man would stand, ankle-deep in mud, watching from the shadows? She stood a moment then, sick with fright, she plunged after her friend.

Sally reached the foot of the slope and started across the soft margin of the hollow, making for the fallen tree. She zig-zagged, hopping from tussock to tussock to avoid the mud. 'Where is he, Meg?' she flung back. 'Where's this funny man of yours, eh?'

Meg slithered the last steep foot and leapt for a tussock.

'Stop, you idiot!' she cried. 'He's there in front of you – look!'

Sally stopped, teetering on a mound with arms outstretched, laughing. 'Where?' She made an exaggerated show of peering into the tangle. 'Who is he, Meg: the Invisible Man?'

Meg made a sideways leap. Under the trees the pattern of light and shadow shifted and the lurking figure came full in view. She saw its face and cried out in revulsion, for it was nothing more than a stiff, livid mask out of which started a pair of lidless, milky eyes.

She turned and ran. Whether Sally followed she neither knew nor cared. She fled gasping: tripped by hummocks, plunging regardless through troughs of greenish, stinking mire, She sobbed as she ran, great choking sobs of horror and of fear. She reached the foot of the slope and skidded and clawed her way up it till she reached the path. Only there did she pause to look back. Sally, mud-smeared down one side, was halfway up. Meg stood gasping and gazing down on the hollow where nothing moved, till her friend reached the path. They ran on, pelting through the twilit wood till the path crossed through a gateway and on across a meadow to the road.

When they reached the road they stopped, leaning on one of a pair of granite gateposts, looking back. The wood was a dark stain against the pinkish sky. As soon as she had breath enough, Sally said, 'What was it, for heaven's sake: what did you see?'

Meg shuddered and shook her head. She didn't want to talk about it. She wanted desperately to blot it out, that ghastly face that floated still before her eyes, but she knew that she could not – that she would be haunted by it for the rest of her life.

'I'm – not sure, Sal,' she whispered. 'I thought it was a man, but if you didn't see it I don't know what it was.'

Sally pulled a face. 'Well I didn't see anything Meg – honestly. Nothing at all. Are you sure it wasn't just shadows or an old stump or something?'

Meg shuddered again. 'It wasn't anything like that, Sal: I wish it was. It had a face – a horrible, blind face and a sort of leather cap. I think it was a ghost.'

Sally made a scornful noise. 'A ghost? There aren't any ghosts, Meg.'

Meg chewed her lip, gazing down at her filthy shoes. She almost said, 'Aren't there, Sal: then what is it that comes to my room sometimes, at night?' but she knew she mustn't. She'd have to explain all about her real grandad – how he disappeared in the war and all that. Sally didn't know about that. She thought Meg's step-grandad was her real one, and Meg didn't feel like going into it so she said, 'Just look at my shoes. Mum'll kill me.'

Sally spread her arms, looking down at herself. 'That's nothing – look at me!' Her right side was a mass of drying mud: the sleeve of her anorak, her skirt and the outside of her leg.

Compared to Sally, Meg had got off lightly, but if she could have swapped places with her friend at that moment, she would gladly have done so: Sal's mud in exchange for the memory of that face. She shivered and said, 'Come on: it's nearly twenty to five. Might as well get it over.' Sally nodded gloomily, and the two girls began walking home through the twilight.

Five

'Where on earth have you been, Meg?' Her mother left off slicing tomatoes to look her up and down. 'I ask you to come straight home and you turn up at ten to five looking like something the cat brought in. I've been worried sick.'

'Sorry, Mum. Sal and I just popped into Judy Woods to see if anything was happening yet.'

'And something obviously was,' observed her mother, tartly. 'A stampede of buffaloes by the look of it. How did you get yourself into that state, girl?'

'Oh . . .' Meg shrugged and pulled a wry face. 'There was this place – a banking, churned up all to mud with motorbikes. We slipped on it and fell.' She didn't usually tell lies but she knew it would be no use telling the truth on this occasion. Her mother would never believe her and besides, it wasn't really a lie: they had slipped and fallen on that slope.

Her mother tipped tomato slices into the salad bowl. 'I wish you'd stay away from Judy Woods, Meg,' she said. 'There are . . .'

'Funny people about, I know,' broke in Meg. 'Funnier than you think,' she murmured, shivering.

Her mother glanced at her. 'What was that you said, dear?'

'Nothing. Sal was with me you know: we were quite safe. Can I wash and change and do something with these shoes now, Mum?'

Her mother nodded. 'I think you'd better, my girl, before your father gets home.' She looked at the kitchen clock. 'Hurry: you've got twenty-five minutes.'

It took Meg a long time to get to sleep that night and when she did she dreamt she was running, running down endless forest aisles in a futile bid to hide herself from milky, sightless eyes.

Six

'Council's approved that nature park thing.' It was Thursday evening and Mr Raven was reading his free copy of the Star. Everybody who worked on the Star got a free copy.

'Oh, yes?' said his wife, vaguely. She was trying to watch *Sixty Minutes* on T.V. Meg was on her way to the kitchen with a stack of dishes. She paused in the doorway to listen.

'Yes. Meeting was last night. All three parties backed the scheme and work's to begin as soon as possible.'

'Ooh, great!' cried Meg. 'School closes for the Easter hols next week – d'you think it'll be started by then, Dad?'

Her father shook his head. 'Doubt it, love. It says here that some of the villagers have formed a group to fight the scheme. The Judy Woods Preservation Society, they're calling themselves. Your grandad's secretary of it.'

'Oh, he would be, wouldn't he?' Mrs Raven leaned forward and turned down the volume. 'Anything awkward: anything that gets in people's way and you can be pretty sure you'll find Henry Boyle at the back of it somewhere.' She looked at her husband. 'And he's not Meg's grandad, Len – only her step-grandad.'

Mr Raven sighed. 'Yes, dear, you keep saying so, but he's married to your mother so he's grandfather to your children whether you like it or not. You're right about the rest, though: he is an awkward old so-and-so.'

'Grandma was on about that on Monday,' put in Meg. 'What'll happen, Dad – will there be marches and sit-ins and things?'

Her father shrugged. 'I don't know, Meg. I expect the Society will seek a meeting with the Council first to puts its point of view. Everybody has a right to his point of view.'

'Point of view?' hooted Mrs Raven. 'If they decided to give

everybody a million pounds, Henry Boyle would start a society to demand two million. He's nothing but a troublemaker and it's time he retired to his garden and kept his nose out of things that don't concern him.'

Meg slipped away to the kitchen. She wished she had ordinary grandparents like Sally, or that Mum would leave off Grandad. After all, she thought, he had been married to Grandma since Mum was a baby – her real father had vanished in his bomber when Mum was eight months old so she couldn't possibly remember him. Hanlon, he'd been called. Michael Hanlon, air-gunner. She wondered what *he* thought of Henry Boyle.

That night he came to her again. She whispered 'Grandad?' but he made no reply as usual. Everything was as usual in fact, except that just as he was fading, he made a gesture towards the window with his hand and shook his head. Meg didn't know how to respond so she merely shrugged under the bedclothes and made an apologetic face.

When he'd gone, the man she'd seen in the woods came into her mind and when she went to sleep she dreamt he pursued her again. She slept fretfully and woke at dawn with a phrase echoing in her head. She tried it on her lips, though it made no sense to her. '*Baby lock you*,' she whispered. '*Baby lock you*.' It seemed to her vitally important, in that instant of waking, to commit these words to memory but when she tried to recall them at breakfast, they had gone.

Seven

'What shall we do tomorrow?' asked Meg. It was Friday teatime. Meg and Sally were standing at the bottom of Newside Road. Behind them, groups of children dawdled homeward on High Street, laughing and making plans for the weekend. Sally pulled a face.

'I dunno. I'd like to go in the woods again but I'm not sure if I dare. I got into terrible trouble on Monday you know – that anorak's not washable and Mum's making me pay for its cleaning out of my own money.'

'I know.' Meg was looking down, moving a little pile of gravel about with the side of her foot. 'Still.' She looked up, grinning. 'We can wear any old tat tomorrow, can't we: and we'll have hours and hours, instead of having to dash in and out before dark.'

Sally nodded. 'I suppose so.' Her eyes met Meg's and she added, 'What about that thing you saw – your ghost or whatever it was? Aren't you bothered about it anymore?'

Meg scraped the gravel into a miniature dune. Without looking up she murmured, 'Sure, I'm bothered, Sal. I had this rotten dream last night. A nightmare. I dreamt he was chasing me through the woods, only it wasn't Judy Woods. It was a forest that went on and on, and he was sort of up in the air behind me – just his face, staring down through the trees with those horrible white eyes, and I couldn't leave him behind no matter now fast I ran.'

'Well.' Sally shrugged. 'Don't you want to keep away, then?'

'Not specially. We don't have to go to Boggy Hollow and I don't suppose I'll see him again. Besides, there'll be other people there tomorrow. What time shall I call for you?'

'Half nine,' said Sally. They parted, and Meg made her way home.

Eight

There had been a touch of frost overnight and the two girls could see their breath as they walked along the road and turned in between the granite gateposts. The sky was clear and bright and the grass beside the path was spangled with the dew.

'I wonder who put those flipping-great gateposts in the hedge like that?' said Sally. 'They look really daft to me. I mean, you'd expect one of those very long driveways with a mansion at the end, instead of a squidgy footpath leading to the woods. It must have been a madman or something.'

Meg shook her head. 'No it wasn't. There was a big house in the olden days. My gran told me. It was where the school is now, and all this land belonged to it. Judy Woods was private, and the people who lived in the house used to shoot pheasants there.'

'Wow!' Sally looked about her. 'All this, somebody's garden – and a whole wood to yourself. When I grow up I'm going to get a place like this. I'll have a goldfish-pond and a herd of deer, and you can come and live with me and we'll play tennis and have tea on the lawn.'

She spoke in a la-di-da voice, and Meg laughed. 'Oh, yes,' she said. 'I can just see it. Us in our anoraks and scruffy jeans, ordering the servants about. "I say, James: do get a move on with that pheasant on toast. And tell Mrs Bridges to give us a shout when John Craven's Newsround comes on".' They minced through the gateway into the wood, twirling imaginary parasols and hooting with mirth.

It was early – not yet ten, and nobody else was in the wood. Birds crashed about in last year's leaves seeking nest materials and rose, fluttering through swelling buds with beaksful of twigs. When Meg and Sally had gone a little way along the footpath Meg said, 'There's still nothing happening, Sal. D'you want to play here, or shall we go back and see who's in the park?' She had been startled a couple of times by rustlings close at hand, and was feeling more nervous than she'd thought she would. Sally shook her head.

'No, Meg. I don't fancy the park any more. It's always full of little kids. Anyway, you said we'd have hours and hours here today. If we hang about a bit, maybe somebody will come.' She grinned. 'The Judy Woods Preservation Society might come and chain themselves to the trees or something and then we could . . .'

'Sssh!' Meg made an urgent gesture and stood with her head on one side, listening. 'I can hear a motor.'

Sally listened. A thin droning sound swelled and faded and swelled again. 'Could be a saw,' she murmured. 'One of those petrol ones. Perhaps they're cutting down trees to make room for the cafe or something. It's coming from over there.'

'No.' Meg shook her head. 'It's behind us, and it's not a saw. It's motor-bikes. It's the bike boys from York.' She nodded towards the trees. 'Come on: we'd better vanish till they've gone past.'

'What for?' Meg had moved to the edge of the path but Sally stayed where she was. 'They're only lads on bikes. They won't do anything to us.'

'You don't know,' said Meg. 'My dad says they're vandals. They wear dirty clothes and swear. Mr Wilson won't let them in the Fox. Come on, Sal.'

Sally shook her head. 'No. You go if you like. You always seem to be running away these days. I'm going to ask them what they think of this being turned into a nature park.'

'You're crazy,' Meg told her. 'What do you expect them to think – they won't be allowed to ride here any more. You'll probably get a smack in the mouth for asking.'

As the girls argued, the engine noise grew to a roar. Meg was about to run into the trees when the first machine came slanting round the bend. She knew that if they saw her running away the boys might make a game of pursuing her so she stood still, groaning inwardly as four more bikes came in view.

The first rider saw Sally standing in the middle of the footpath. He rode straight at her and swerved at the very last instant, bringing his machine to a skidding halt. He was encased from neck to feet in black leather and wore a scarlet helmet on his head. Across the front of the helmet, above the visor, the word 'Radar' had been painted in black. As the other machines came popping and snarling round, he flicked up his visor and looked at Sally.

'What the heck d'you think you're on, kiddo – standing in the middle of the road like that. Trying to get yourself killed or summat?'

Sally gazed back at him. 'It's not a road,' she said coolly, 'it's a footpath, and it's you who shouldn't be on it, not me.'

'Whoo – hoo!' The boy twisted in the saddle, appealing to his companions. 'D'you hear that, lads? We shouldn't be here. Maybe we'd better split before Wonder Woman here takes us apart.'

The four youths, astraddle their machines, gazed coldly at the girl from beneath their visors. 'Don't look like no Wonder Woman to me, Radar,' one of them drawled. 'Looks more like some cheeky little kid. Tie her behind your bike and drag her to death.'

'No!' Meg, who had remained motionless at the edge of the path, stepped forward. 'You can't. You wouldn't dare. You'd get in trouble with the police.'

The boys yelped with laughter. One of them threw up his arms to shield his face. 'Not the police!' he begged. 'Anything but the police.'

'Aaagh!' screamed Radar, pretending to cower. 'First Wonder Woman, now Supergran – save me, somebody!'

Stung by their mockery, Meg blurted, 'Go on then – have a good laugh. You won't be laughing when there's a warden here to keep you out though, will you?'

The youths hung over their petrol-tanks, helpless with mirth. Radar wiped his streaming eyes with the back of a gauntlet and said, still laughing, 'Warden: what warden? What you on about, kid?'

'This,' put in Sally. 'Judy Woods. Haven't you heard – they're making it into a nature park.'

Radar stopped laughing. He blinked like an owl and said, 'You're joking.' Both girls shook their heads.

'It's not a joke,' said Meg. 'It's been in the paper. We came to see if they'd started work yet but they haven't.'

Radar gazed at her blankly and said, 'Hey lads: shurrup a minute and listen, will you?' His companions fell silent and he went on, 'Say that again, kiddo.'

The boys gazed at Meg through hostile eyes. She swallowed and said, 'They're turning these woods into a nature park and leisure reserve. It was in the paper.'

The youths looked at one another, then at their leader. One of them said, 'So what?'

Radar gave him a contemptuous glance. 'They're having a warden, you dummy, that's what. A warden, with a dirty great alsatian or summat to see us off if we come biking. Where we gonna ride if not here, eh?' He turned back to the girls. 'Well they're flippin' not, I can tell you that!' he snarled. 'This is our scramble-track and nobody's kicking us off it. There's fifty of us when we're all here, and if they try keeping us out there'll be trouble: big trouble. Come on!'

He slammed down his visor and gunned his engine. The motorbike leapt forward and Sally had to step back quickly to keep from being hit. The others followed, swerving and roaring away, leaving the two girls in a cloud of blue smoke.

'Pooh!' Meg coughed and gazed after the bikes, fanning herself with her hand. 'What a stink and what a row. I told you to come away, didn't I?'

Sally shrugged. 'I like the smell of motorbikes,' she said. 'And they didn't hurt us, did they – I knew they wouldn't.'

'That first one nearly knocked you over!' retorted Meg. 'That Radar or whatever he calls himself. Radar! What sort of a stupid name's that, anyway?'

Sally grinned. 'He was quite nice really,' she said. 'I wouldn't mind a ride on the back of his bike.'

Meg looked at her friend and shook her head. 'You're crazy, Sal,' she said. 'He's a vandal, and it sounds to me as though he's going to start a fight or something. I wish we hadn't told him about the nature park.'

'He'd have found out anyway,' said Sally. 'And besides, I hope he does start something.' She nudged Meg, her eyes shining. 'At least it won't be boring!'

Nine

When Meg woke on Sunday morning, she thought she remembered seeing her grandad sometime during the night. Then she realised it couldn't have been Grandad because Grandad had no moustache, whereas the dark figure she'd seen had. The whole thing was very hazy though, and after thinking about it for a while she decided she must have dreamt it. The odd thing was, she'd remembered those words she'd tried so hard to recall on Friday. *Baby lock you.* And now there was another – *jubilee*.

She sat up, opened the drawer of her bedside cabinet and rummaged about, whispering the words so as not to lose them again. She found an old felt-tip and, by pressing on, managed to scrawl them in orange on the back of a Christmas card she'd saved.

Sunday was lying-in morning for the Ravens. Nobody stirred till nine, when Dad usually got up and made everybody's breakfast. The delicious aromas of coffee and bacon would then rouse everybody else and there would be a long, leisurely breakfast: what Mrs Raven called a family breakfast, with conversation and fat Sunday papers. Meg often thought how nice it would be if they could get up at nine every morning, instead of grumping and snapping at one another all week in the pale dawn.

She put the pen and card on the cabinet and squinted at the little travelling clock. Ten to eight. Ages yet. She snuggled down and pulled up the covers.

Baby lock you. The meaningless phrase kept repeating itself in her mind, over and over. *Baby lock you. Jubilee.* She tried to go back to sleep but her brain wouldn't let her. It seemed to her that the words were linked in some way to the faces she'd seen, or thought she'd seen, but she didn't know how. *Baby lock you*. She'd dreamt of the white-eyed man and woken with those words in her head. And now *jubilee*, and a moustachioed man. Perhaps she was going mad.

She slept eventually and woke to the sounds and smells of breakfast. She had forgotten what it was she'd been worrying about, and might have got through the day without giving the strange words another thought if she hadn't written them on that card. As it was, she saw them the instant she swung her legs out of bed, and caught herself whispering them over and over again as she washed and dressed.

It was no fun, she decided. Definitely no fun. The word obsession occurred to her. There'd been this film on T.V. – oh, ages ago now, called Obsession. She'd asked Dad what it meant and he'd said obsession was when somebody thinks about one thing all the time – it might be food or football or murder – anything. He thinks about it so much there's no room in his mind for anything else at all and he can't run his life and ends up a weirdo. Meg wondered if she was becoming obsessed with her dreams. Had she really seen that frightful thing in Boggy Hollow or was she crazy already or what? Sal hadn't seen it.

Meg contributed little to the breakfast-time conversation that morning. She was so quiet, and looked so pale that her mother kept watching her when she thought Meg wasn't looking. She noted the blue-black smudges under her daughter's eyes and a faintly worried expression settled on her face.

Presently, Paul and his father excused themselves and went outside to wash the car. Mrs Raven leaned forward and caught Meg's eye.

'Is everything all right, dear?'

'Sure,' said Meg. 'Why?'

'You're very quiet and there are dark rings under your eyes. You don't feel ill or anything, do you?'

'No Mum,' Meg murmured. 'I don't feel ill. Or anything. I've been having dreams, that's all. Nightmares really. I can't sleep, and I'm starting to think about them in the daytime. I think I'm obsessed.'

Mrs Raven laughed briefly. 'Obsessed? Now what on earth would a child your age be obsessed about: is something the

26

matter at school, Meg?' Meg shook her head. She wanted to talk, but she was afraid her mother would laugh at her or get mad.

'It's the dreams,' she said. 'There's these two men – one with a moustache and one with funny eyes.'

'Sounds like Laurel and Hardy,' said Mrs Raven brightly. Meg shot her a distressed look and she said, 'Sorry dear: go on.'

'There's these two men.' Meg's eyes were downcast and she twisted her fingers in her lap as she spoke. 'One chases me. The other stands looking down at me in bed. And in the morning I'm thinking some words to myself and I know they're daft but I can't get them out of my head.' She stopped, looking down at her hands. Mrs Raven leaned forward across the table.

'What are these words, Meg: can you remember them now?'

Meg nodded. 'Yes. I wrote them down. They're "baby lock you", and "jubilee".' She looked up, a plea in her eyes. 'Do they make sense to you, Mum?'

Mrs Raven shook her head. 'No, Meg – I'm afraid they don't.' She regarded her daughter gravely. 'You know Meg, when you were very small you used to say that Grandad came and looked at you in your bed. Daddy and I told you time and time again what nonsense it was, but you persisted in your little fantasy. We became quite worried about you: so worried that we very nearly took you to the doctor but then, quite suddenly, you grew tired of pretending and we heard no more about it.' She stood up and began gathering up crockery. 'Dreams are nonsense, dear,' she went on, 'and you must put them out of your mind.' She smiled. 'Otherwise, we might have to think about taking you to the doctor after all.'

Meg said nothing. She wanted to say, 'He still comes. He always has, and now there are others, unless I'm going crazy. And that's what I want to know, Mum: am I going mad? I'm frightened and I need your help and yes, maybe you should take me to the doctor.' She wanted to say something like that, but she knew it would only make her mother angry. Mum was all right if you had flu or a cut finger or a headache, but if you were simply fed-up or scared or something she thought you

27

were being weak and silly and that if she became angry and snapped at you, you'd stop your nonsense and everything would be all right.

Everything was not all right. Meg felt scared in a vague sort of way and the day was spoilt for her. It wasn't a bad day. The sun shone, and she and Sally went to the woods before lunch and to the park after, but her heart wasn't in it. At one point, Sally looked at her and said, 'What's up, Meg?' and she forced a smile and said, 'Nothing, Sal.' She didn't feel like talking to Sally about it. She wanted to talk to her grandma, but she'd have to wait till tomorrow for that. Grandma went to church twice on Sundays and baked and cleaned in between so she couldn't do with callers.

As it grew dark, Meg's uneasiness increased and when it was bedtime, she didn't want to go up. When she did go, she lay awake for a long time, listening to the muffled sound of the T.V. downstairs, and her parents' voices. She gazed into the dark corners of her room but nothing stirred. After a long time she heard Paul coming up, which meant it was ten o'clock, and soon after that she fell asleep. She never heard her parents climb the stairs, and when she woke up it was morning.

Ten

It was the last week of school and they were doing exams. On Friday they would break up for Easter. Everybody was looking forward to it. Meg wasn't brilliant at school but she liked exams and Monday morning passed like a flash. It was English. They had to write an essay describing a favourite place and Meg wrote about the riverbank at York: the boats and the trees and the tourists in bright clothes, sitting at little tables near the water. She was good at this sort of thing, and she was so absorbed in her writing that she hadn't time to brood about her fears. Before she knew, the bell went and Mr Parker collected up the papers and she was outside, walking towards her grandma's house.

She waited till they'd finished lunch then said, 'Grandma – do you ever have frightening dreams?' Her grandad was at the Fox and the two of them were sitting over cups of tea. The old lady smiled. 'Yes, Meg. Sometimes. I think everybody does. Why?'

Meg pulled a face. 'Oh: I've been having them lately and I can't talk to Mum. She says dreams are rubbish and I've got to stop worrying about them but I can't.'

Her grandmother nodded. 'I know,' she said. 'Your mum believes in what she can see, and everything else is nonsense. That's why she stopped going to church. Tell me about your dreams. Are they always the same ones?'

Meg shook her head. 'Not quite.' She told her about the two men. When she'd finished her grandmother said, 'And are they like people you know – teachers at school perhaps?'

Meg shook her head. 'No. I've never seen them before. Except . . .'

The old lady looked at Meg over the rim of her cup. 'Except what, dear?'

29

Meg looked down, rotating her cup in its saucer. 'Except I thought I saw the blind one in Boggy Hollow the other day. I was with Sal but she couldn't see him. I'm scared I might be going mad.'

'Oh no, dear!' Her grandmother leaned across the table and laid a hand on Meg's. 'You mustn't think like that. Lots of people have the same dream over and over again. It doesn't mean they're mad.'

Meg looked down at the wrinkled hand. 'There are some words too.'

'Words?'

'Yes. I wake up with words in my head and they don't make sense.'

'Do the men say these words, Meg?'

'No. They're in my mind when I wake up.'

'Say them to me.'

Meg hesitated. 'You'll think I'm daft.'

'No I shan't dear – I promise.' She squeezed Meg's hand.

Meg smiled faintly. 'All right. It's "baby lock you", and "jubilee".'

The old lady made a noise in her throat and Meg shrugged. 'I told you they didn't make sense, didn't I?'

Her grandmother made no reply but withdrew her hand from Meg's and sat gazing at the tablecloth with an odd expression on her face.

Meg waited, feeling she must have offended her in some way. After a moment she murmured, 'What's wrong, Grandma – did I say something wrong?'

There was a silence, during which the old lady stared at her hands. Red, shiny hands with square nails and a thin gold ring. She shook her head slightly and whispered, 'No. No, you didn't say anything wrong, Meg. Say the words again, please.'

' "Baby lock you", and "jubilee".'

Her grandmother nodded. 'Yes. There weren't any others, I suppose?'

'Others?'

'Other words?'

'No. Not that I remember. Do they make sense to you, Grandma?'

The old lady shook her head. 'I'm not sure, Meg. It depends. It's either a fantastic coincidence, or –' She hesitated. 'Look, Meg. I don't want to say anything just yet. I need time to think. I'm sorry if I'm not being much help, but you've given me a bit of a jolt I'm afraid. One thing's certain though.' She covered Meg's hand again and smiled. 'You're not going mad, so you can forget any worries in that direction and we'll talk about it again tomorrow. All right, dear?'

Meg nodded. 'All right, Grandma. I feel tons better anyway. I knew you'd listen.'

'Yes, well.' The old lady smiled. 'It's one of the few things we old crocks are good for, listening. It's ten past one now, so you'd better run along and I'll see you tomorrow.'

Meg set off back to school. She was even more puzzled than she'd been before, but not nearly so worried somehow. She even hummed to herself as she walked along the road.

Eleven

At teatime, Paul said, 'We start work on Judy Woods a week today.'

Mrs Raven smiled. 'So it is your group that will do the job,' she said. 'That's lovely. You'll be able to pop home at lunchtimes if you want to.'

'Big deal,' growled her son.

'Yes,' put in Meg. 'But what about the Judy Woods Preservation Society?'

'Stirrer,' said Paul.

'There's a bit in the paper about it,' said Mr Raven. 'The Society demanded a public inquiry but it was turned down. The place is supposed to have been surveyed today and work starts next Monday. They interviewed your grandad. Just a minute.' He rattled the paper and adjusted his glasses. 'Yes – here it is. Mr Henry Boyle, Secretary of the Judy Woods Preservation Society told our reporter, "It's disgraceful. Most people in Wilberforce are behind us in our campaign to stop this interference with a local beauty-spot, and to deny them a public inquiry is undemocratic. If the Council thinks it's heard the last of us, it's mistaken. We shall fight on, and we shall win, however long it takes." '

'Good old Henry!' cried Paul. 'I hope he does come and fight. It'll be more fun than humping old mattresses about.'

His mother made a scornful noise. 'Silly old goat!' she said. 'What does he imagine he can do – him and his ridiculous Society? It's a sheer lie to say most people in Wilberforce are behind him. Everybody I know is dying for the place to be cleaned up.'

'Yes.' Mr Raven folded the paper and poured himself another cup of tea. 'It is a bit much, calling Judy Woods a local beauty-spot. It might be a beauty-spot when Paul and his friends are done with it, but it certainly isn't now.'

'We might never be done with it,' grinned Paul. 'Henry's commandos might ambush us and mow us down with machine-gun fire.'

'We can always hope,' growled Meg. 'May I leave the table, Mum?'

'No,' her brother snapped. 'Get it eaten.'

It was a chilly evening. Meg zipped up her jacket and hurried along the road. When she got to Sally's house, Mrs Barnet answered the door. 'Sally's staying in tonight, Meg,' she said. 'It's the maths exam tomorrow and her dad's giving her some practice.'

'Oh, okay, Mrs Barnet,' said Meg. 'Thanks.' She was disappointed. She didn't fancy going into the woods alone but it couldn't be helped. If the place had been surveyed like it said in the paper, there might be something to see and she wasn't going to miss it.

She turned in between the granite gateposts and glanced at her watch. Twenty past six. The sun was low but it wouldn't set for over an hour yet. Plenty of time. She glanced towards the trees, shivered, and set off across the field.

As soon as she reached the gateway into the wood, she knew that somebody had been here. The gap in the dilapidated fence was partly blocked by clumps of little trees which had sprung up in recent years. These trees now had black crosses painted on them, and Meg guessed they were to be cut down. She passed through the gateway. It was dim under the trees, but as soon as she was inside she knew she wouldn't have to look any further.

To the right of the footpath, oaks and sycamores grew thinly on an expanse of level ground, and this ground was now marked out for building. Stakes had been hammered in and pink tape had been stretched from stake to stake to show where foundations would be dug and drains laid. Meg left the path and went and stood among the stakes and tapes and tried to make out the positions and shapes of the buildings, but she couldn't. It was like being inside one of those maze puzzles where you have to find your way from the edge to the centre without crossing any lines.

She was making her way back to the path when she heard

motorbikes. She gasped, and started to run towards the gateway. Then she realised that the machines must already be crossing the field. If she left that way she'd be seen. She glanced about her for somewhere to hide. The buds had not yet burst and you could see for miles through the wood. Meg had just decided she'd have to make a dash for the first bend in the path when she saw the holly tree. It was only a bush really – a squat, dark shape twenty yards away, but it was thick with leaves that would hide her. She sprinted towards it, swerving between the sycamores, praying that she'd reach it before the first bike came in sight.

She made it, but only just, skidding to a crouching halt as, with a throaty roar, Radar's machine came hurtling through the gap. It was followed at once by another, and then a third and a fourth and a fifth. Radar had seen the stakes. Without slowing, he swung his bike off the path and went weaving through the trees. The others followed. There were eight now, and as Meg squinted through the foliage two more came in sight. She crouched motionless, wishing she was doing maths at home. Ten bikes. Ten. They filled the sky with roaring and with acrid, blue exhaust.

Radar drove straight at the tape which stretched, dragged a stake from the ground then snapped, wrapping itself round the bike. The boy rode on, dragging the tape and stake behind him like a tail. The others followed – reaching down, wrenching up stakes and brandishing them with wild cries. Weaving through the trees with long pink ribbons streaming out behind. One lad rode round and round a single tree, wrapping it in ribbon till it looked like a crude maypole. In less than two minutes, the site was reduced to a shambles of uprooted stakes, festoons of dirty tape, and mud. As Meg watched, Radar raised a gauntlet, shouted an order and led his riders bouncing and skidding back to the path and away.

Meg waited in case any of the riders returned, but the engine-noise receded towards the road and after a moment she straightened up and came out from behind the bush. She walked along the path and stood gazing at the wrecked site. She didn't know what to do. She'd witnessed an offence. She ought to tell the police but she didn't want to. What Radar and his friends had done was wrong, and yet Meg could see why they'd done it. Nobody likes bike-boys. Their noisy machines upset people and their riding-gear gets them barred from coffee-bars and discos. They're supposed to be a menace on the roads and yet, whenever they find themselves a quiet place to ride, somebody drives them away. It's like gypsies. Everybody thinks they should go somewhere else.

She decided not to say anything. If challenged, she would say the damage had already been done when she got there. Nobody was going to know.

She turned towards the gateway, and almost cried out. A man was watching her from the shadows.

Twelve

She would run as she did in dreams, uselessly through the dim wood and he would follow, only this time there would be no awakening. This time . . . She was about to run when a voice said, 'Hold on lass – I'll not hurt you.' The voice was surly but it was known to Meg and she turned, weak with relief. Dan Stamper stepped forward so that what was left of the light fell on his face. It was long and brown and deeply seamed, with pale blue shifty eyes and a rime of silver stubble. The mouth had a twist to it and this, together with those eyes, gave the old fellow a crafty look which exactly matched his character.

Dan Stamper was not a popular man. Tight with his money and caring nothing for the welfare of others, he was rumoured to have a fortune hidden away somewhere on the rundown farm beyond the wood where he lived alone. Mostly, he kept himself to himself. When he came into the village he came on foot and if he slipped into the Fox for a drink, he drank alone. A large dog patrolled his dilapidated property at all times and its ferocious barking kept would-be callers from his door. Now, he nodded towards the damaged site and said, 'Who did this?'

Meg shrugged. 'I – don't know, Mr Stamper. It was done when I got here.' The old man spat on the ground.

'Like fun it was. I watched you walk into this wood and I saw the motorbikes arrive. I reckon you know 'em. I reckon you arranged to meet 'em here. What's their names, eh? That one with the red helmet for instance.'

Meg bit her lip. She was a bit scared of old Stamper. All the kids were. Desperate Dan they called him, but not to his face. There was a story that he kept a kid in a chicken-coop at the farm. He'd caught him on his land and locked him up, and now he beat him every day and gave him henfood to eat.

This kid had been so long with the chickens he'd forgotten how to talk. He clucked and flapped his arms like wings. Meg didn't believe the story but she was scared just the same.

'I don't know them, Mr Stamper,' she said. 'Honestly. I wouldn't help them to do a thing like this anyway – I want the nature park built.'

'Oh you do, do you?' growled Stamper. 'Well I don't see?' He spat again. 'Hordes of ruddy townies all over the place, leaving gates open and breaking walls down. But I've no time for these louts on motorbikes either, and if I get to know who they are I'll have the law on 'em: understand?'

Meg nodded. She wanted to say that he was an idle old devil and that most of his gates and walls had fallen down from neglect, but she didn't. It was nearly dark and she wanted to be out of the wood. She walked round the old man, making for the gateway. He didn't move, but called after her as she started across the field.

'There'll be no nature park here while I'm alive so you can just keep away, and tell them ruddy teddy-boys to keep away and all!'

'Teddy-boys!' Meg muttered to herself as she walked away. 'Silly old fool.' Then she remembered how glad she'd been to hear his voice and she shivered and quickened her pace.

Thirteen

When Meg got home, Paul was out and her parents were watching a film. She didn't say anything, but fetched herself biscuits and milk from the kitchen and sat for a while, munching and watching. It was a Dustin Hoffman film. His wife had left him and he was trying to look after their little boy and do his job at the same time. The kid was spoilt and whiny and didn't seem to realise how lucky he was to be with Dustin Hoffman. He got on Meg's nerves. At half past eight she finished her milk, excused herself and went to bed. Maybe if she got an early night she'd do all right in the maths exam tomorrow.

As soon as she got herself tucked in she started thinking about her grandmother's odd behaviour at dinnertime. The old lady had acted as if those dream words had meant something to her but Meg didn't see how they could. 'You've given me a bit of a jolt,' she'd said. Meg whispered the words and began turning them over and over inside her head and the next thing she knew, she'd been asleep and it was the middle of the night and there was something in the room.

She smelled it first. A smell like – like burning. She lay with a pounding heart and the covers pulled up to her chin, straining her eyes into the darkness, wondering what had woken her. She couldn't even make out the window. There was only blackness, except for the faint green luminescence of the clock and, when she raised her head a little, a pale streak under her door.

Something was in the room. An unseen presence and a smell of burning where no fire was. On her cabinet stood a lamp with a little switch, only it was a top-heavy lamp and you had to put your hand right up inside the shade to get at the switch and unless you were very careful you'd knock the shade and the whole thing would go crashing over and the silence would be shattered and who could tell what would happen then? She knew she must not break the silence, unless she could guarantee to replace it instantly with light. The silence was keeping everything where it was. If the silence broke, something might launch itself at her through the break and only instant light would save her then.

Silently, she eased her left arm from under the covers and extended her hand, using the glow from the clock as a guide. When her hand eclipsed the glow, she reached up and back, very slowly, hoping the bed wouldn't creak. Her eyes shifted from the green luminescence to the blackness around her and back again, and her scalp prickled when she thought of something suddenly grabbing her hand.

Up, and back. Her arm ached. Surely her groping hand had somehow missed the lamp? But no – there it was, cold against the knuckle of her little finger. Steady then – back off a fraction and turn the hand, slowly; feel for it with the fingertips. There. Up now – slide them up, ever so gently and mind that stupid shade. There's its rim now, tickling the back of the wrist, so stop. Stop. The slightest knock and it's over. Move the fingers only. Feel for that switch – there! There it is. Now – get the thumb over it and curl the fingers round the back so you're squeezing, not pushing. Ready – go!

Light filled the room – the instant light she'd wanted but it couldn't save her. It fell upon his face and yet for him the room stayed black, for he was blind.

Fourteen

He was between the wardrobe and the chair and it was him
– the man from Boggy Hollow. Meg saw milky, hideous eyes
and charred clothing and recoiled with a cry. The lamp toppled
and went out. She began to scream. Clumsy footfalls thudded
over the carpet. She flung herself shrieking across the bed, and
felt herself held.

'Meg – come on love. It's all right. I've got you.' She opened
her eyes, squinting against the light. Her father was sitting on
the bed in pyjamas, his hands gripping her shoulders. Behind
him hovered her mother, looking down at her with anxious
eyes.

'All right now?' said her father, softly. She shook her head.

'No.' She was trembling, and so damp that her nightie stuck
to her body when she moved. She lifted her head. 'Where is
he?'

'Who, love?' Her father laid a cool hand on her forehead,
gently pushed her back on to the pillow and stroked her hair.

'Him – the blind man. He was over there by the wardrobe.'

Her father smiled. 'There was nobody, Meg,' he said. 'You
had a nightmare but it's over now.'

'Scared us half to death,' said her mother, 'screaming like
that. And just look what you've done to your lamp.'

'Yes well – never mind that now, love,' said Mr Raven.
'Would you like the light left on, Meg, or are you all right
now?'

Meg shook her head. 'I want it on. There was somebody
here, Dad, honestly. I wasn't asleep.'

'It sometimes seems like that,' said her father. 'Many a time
I could have sworn somebody's said something to me at work,
but then it's turned out I dreamt it.' He stood up. 'I'll leave
the light on, then.' He picked up the fallen lamp and frowned.

'Hmm: too easily upset, this thing. Bulb's gone by the look of it.' He turned it in his hand. 'P'raps I could put some sort of weight in the bottom here – make it more stable, and in the meantime we'd better have it unplugged.' He bent and pulled the plug from the wall-socket. 'I don't know much about electricity but I thought I smelled burning when I came in here.'

Fifteen

The maths exam was a disaster. Meg had been awake most of the night and at breakfast her mother mentioned the doctor again. She had arrived at school with a headache, to discover that the exam consisted mostly of stuff she hated and was no good at. She'd stared blankly out of the window, chewing the end of her pencil while next to her, Sally worked like a demon and demolished the paper in twenty minutes flat.

It often seems that when a day begins badly, it continues the same way. Meg spent the whole morning waiting for dinnertime so that she could talk to her grandma, but when she arrived at the cottage in Fox Place her grandad was there. He greeted Meg cheerfully enough, but she caught a glance from the old lady which meant, 'Don't mention you-know-what – not in front of him!'

'Now then, Meg,' said her grandad. 'Exam time, your grandma tells me. How's it going?' Meg pulled a face.

'Okay yesterday, not so good today. Yesterday was English but we had maths today.' The old man chuckled.

'I wasn't so hot at maths myself. Arithmetic, they called it in my day. Come to think of it, I wasn't much good at English either. I was the class dunce really but I'm still here, so it doesn't seem to have done me much harm, does it?'

'Henry!' The old lady frowned at him over her glasses. 'Don't you go putting ideas into Meg's head. School's important – a lot more important than it used to be. You can't get anywhere today without a string of O-levels and what-not.'

'Aye, I know,' growled the old man, stabbing peas with his fork. 'And what do they know, with their O-levels and their A-levels and their flippin' diplomas, eh?' He nodded in the direction of the city. 'Yon shower in t'town hall's got a trunkful of diplomas between 'em, but they know nowt about what's good for folks. Nature parks!' he scoffed. 'Leisure reserves. They'll be wanting to convert the whole cowing village into Disneyland next, I suppose.'

'Henry!' His wife glared. 'Mind your language in front of the child, please.' Old Henry sighed.

'Aye, all right, love, but it drives me wild that's all. Interferin' in folks' lives – they can't leave owt alone.'

Meg felt like telling him the site had been wrecked but she didn't. He'd only start asking questions, and if he didn't her grandma would. Had she seen who'd done it and so on. She said nothing, and the meal proceeded more or less in silence. At five to one, old Henry pushed his pudding dish away, drained his mug and stood up.

'If ye'll excuse me,' he said, 'there's a couple of fellas I've got to see at the Fox.' He put on his jacket and went out of the room. Meg glanced at her grandma but the old lady raised a finger to her lips and shook her head. After a moment her husband's head came round the door.

'I'll be off then,' he said. He winked at Meg and added, 'Do your best with those exams love, but don't worry about 'em – all right?'

Meg smiled and nodded. 'I'll try,' she said.

'That's the ticket.' His head vanished. They sat listening till the front door closed and his footfalls receded down the path. The old lady stared at the tablecloth, her bottom lip caught between her teeth.

'Grandma,' said Meg, 'the blind man was in my room last night. Everybody thinks it was a nightmare but it wasn't. It was real. Even Dad smelled burning.'

Her grandmother glanced up at her. 'Burning?'

'Yes. His clothes were burned. I saw them as plainly as I see you now. What is it, Grandma – what's happening to me? You know, don't you?'

Her grandmother laid a hand over Meg's and squeezed. 'I – think so, Meg, yes.' Her eyes searched the girl's features. 'Tell me: has your mother ever spoken to you about your other grandad. Your real one?' Meg nodded.

'Yes. You know she has. She's told me all about him lots of times.'

The old lady nodded. 'All right. Now I want you to think very carefully, dear. Has she ever mentioned your grandad's friends – the men who flew with him. The men who were with him when he went missing?'

Meg nodded. 'Oh, yes. She says there were seven of them including Grandad, and he was the oldest. She says you told her that.'

'Their names. Has she ever mentioned their names?'

Meg shook her head. 'No. I don't think she knew their names. I mean, she was only a baby, wasn't she? She'd only know them if you told her.'

'I didn't tell her. I'd remember if I had. Has she any snapshots, Meg – photos of your grandad and his crew?'

Meg shook her head again. 'No. Only the one of Grandad. The one on the sideboard. Why are you asking me all these questions?'

Her grandmother squeezed her hand again. 'Because it's important, Meg: more important than you know. You know nothing at all about them, then?'

'Nothing except what I've told you. Why, Grandma?'

The old lady stared at Meg's hand in her own. 'Because you told me two of their names yesterday.'

Meg felt herself go cold. 'How d'you mean?' she gasped. 'You mean two of them were called "baby lock you" and "jubilee"? There's no such names.'

'Oh yes.' The woman nodded. 'There are, Meg. Or rather there were. Lockyer's real name was Douglas. He was a gunner, like your grandad. He was only nineteen so the others called him Baby.' She smiled. 'They were great ones for nicknames, those boys. The other was Arthur Lee. Your grandad called him Juby as a joke. Juby Lee. So there you are.' She gazed into Meg's eyes. 'Now you know why you gave me such a turn yesterday. I've spent every minute since racking my brains, trying to think how you could have known – how their names might have cropped up and been stored away in your subconscious, but they can't have. I lay all night, thinking and thinking, and what I think now is this – that you're getting visits from members of Michael's crew. Why, I don't know. I don't know how to stop it, either, but one thing I'm

44

certain of is that they can't possibly mean you any harm, Meg.'
She pulled a wry face. 'I'm sorry if that's no great comfort but
it's the best I can do. I want us to look at a snapshot in a
minute, but first I have to ask you something.'

She hesitated and Meg said, 'I know what it is, Grandma,
and the answer's yes. I've seen Grandad, lots of times. I
wanted to tell you ages ago but I thought you wouldn't believe
me. Mum doesn't. I daren't even mention the subject in our
house any more.'

The old lady shook her head. 'It's a thing many people can't
accept, Meg. It isn't their fault – they just aren't made that
way. Tell me: what does he look like?'

Meg tilted her head on one side and closed her eyes. 'He's
like his picture,' she said. 'And he nearly always smiles. He
wears this overall thing with lots of straps and buckles. He
only stays a little while and I'm never frightened when he's
there.' She opened her eyes and looked at the old lady. 'Why
me, Grandma?' she said. 'I mean, why does he come to me
and not you? You'd think . . .'

Her grandmother shook her head. 'Who knows, Meg: perhaps you have the gift and I don't. You look like him you
know – that dark hair and those brown eyes. Maybe that's
got something to do with it. Just a minute.' She pushed her
chair back and stood up. 'I don't want to make you late for
school, but I'll fetch that photograph.'

She left the room. Meg sat with her hands wrapped round
her empty cup, staring into it without seeing. She felt numb
and detached as though she were floating in space with everything and everybody else a very long way away. When her
grandmother came back Meg didn't notice, and she started
violently when the album was placed in front of her. The old
lady leaned over her shoulder and tapped a rather blurred
photograph with her fingernail. 'Here – see if you can pick
out your two visitors, Meg.'

Meg looked at the photograph. It was a postcard-size en-
largement of six men standing under the wing of a big aeroplane. They were all grinning, and one was giving the thumbs-
up sign. The photographer's shadow lay on the concrete
in front of them. She studied their faces, wondering if they'd

have smiled like that if they'd known they were going to die.

When her eyes reached the last man on the right, a chill squeezed her heart. She jabbed at the image with her finger.

'That one. He came. I can tell by the moustache.'

'Ah-ha.' Her grandmother's voice sounded strange. 'That confirms it, then. That's Juby Lee. Go on.'

'No.' Meg shook her head. 'I don't know any of the others.' Her forehead was hot and she felt sick.

'What about this one?' The old lady indicated the second face from the left. It was a long, pasty face with deep-set eyes that made it look like a skull in the photograph. Meg shook her head.

'That one's Baby Lockyer,' said her grandmother. 'Your blind man, I think. Something must have . . .'

'Can I have a glass of water, please?'

'Yes dear, of course. I'm sorry.' She shuffled away, fetching a glass; filling it at the tap. Meg took it and sipped the cold water. Her hand shook, so that the rim rattled against her teeth and some of the water slopped into her lap. Her grandmother closed the musty-smelling album and laid a hand on Meg's shoulder.

'I'm sorry dear, really I am. I've been extremely thoughtless and I've made you feel ill. I'll phone the school, and you must stay here this afternoon and rest.'

'No.' Meg put down the glass and shook her head. 'I'm all right now, Grandma, and besides I've got an exam first period. I don't know what it was but it's gone now. I'm glad we had this talk.'

The old lady smiled and shook her head. 'I'm sure I don't know why, Meg, because I've been no help to you. None whatever.'

'Yes you have,' said Meg. 'I know I'm not going crazy now, for one thing. And I know I can always talk to you about my – visitors.' She stood up. 'I'll see you tomorrow, okay?'

The old lady came with her to the door. She was still there when Meg looked back from the corner. They both waved.

Sixteen

The next couple of days passed uneventfully for Meg. She slept badly and felt she must be making a mess of her exams, but there were no further hauntings. On Wednesday, Paul announced that he had been chosen to learn to drive an earth-mover when work began on the Judy Woods project, and on Thursday eleven members of the Preservation Society marched the eight miles to York and sat chanting on the Town Hall steps, the better to rest their blistered feet. At teatime the same day, Meg and Sally went into the wood and found it staked and taped afresh, with the added feature of a watchman in a yellow plastic shelter.

And so Friday came: an end to exams and the start of the Easter holidays. As they filed out of school the children received envelopes containing their end-of-term reports. Meg opened hers on the way home and found she was top in English but nowhere in anything else. In the space marked Science old Moorhouse had scrawled, 'No budding Einstein – Frankenstein more likely.' She'd come nineteenth out of thirty overall. Sally was first.

Her parents made a big thing out of studying the wretched document over the evening meal, clucking and shaking their heads while Paul smirked. 'I don't know what's to become of you, Meg,' her father sighed, 'really I don't.'

'No,' replied Meg, glumly. 'I expect I'll become a tramp or a pickpocket or something. I might even end up driving an earth-mover in Judy Woods.'

As soon as the ghastly meal was over, Meg changed into jeans and a jumper and went off to meet Sally at the bottom of Newside Road. When she arrived, her friend was already there.

'Hey, guess what?' Sally's eyes shone.

'What?'

47

'Dad gave me three pounds for coming top. Look.' She unzipped her shoulder-bag and pulled out three crisp notes.

'Lucky you,' growled Meg. 'All I got was a lecture about pulling my socks up and another about being cheeky.'

'Never mind,' chirped Sally. 'We'll go over there and drink about twenty cokes and play the juke-box.' She nodded towards the little café across the road. The sign above the door said 'Peg's', though the proprietors were in fact called Len and Mabel. In high summer the café sold tea and snacks to what Len called the passing trade, but for the rest of the year it rivalled the youth club as a gathering place for the young people of the village. It had plastic chairs and tables, a single dim striplight which gave the place an agreeably sleazy look, and the only juke-box in Wilberforce. A fading notice in the window read 'No leathers'. Len and Mabel had a thing about motorbikes.

'My dad doesn't like me going in there,' said Meg. 'But then he doesn't like me going anywhere so let's go.' They crossed the road and went into the café. The light was on, though it was still broad daylight outside. Mabel was dusting some glass shelves on the counter. There were no other customers.

'Hi, Mabel,' said Sally. Len and Mabel liked to be called by their first names.

The woman nodded. 'Hello, Sally, Meg. What can I get you?'

'Cokes, please. And can we have some tens in the change?' She put a pound note on the counter.

Mabel pulled a face. 'You're going to start feeding the beast, aren't you?' she said. The beast was her name for the juke-box.

Sally nodded, grinning.

'You bet. And can we have the sound up, please?'

Mabel winced. 'I suppose so. It's your money, though what anybody sees in the rubbish they're bringing out today I don't know. It's not like in my day. They could all play their instruments then, and they could sing and all. Not like this lot, screaming and prancing about while computers do all the work.'

'Computers?' said Meg.

'Aye.' Mabel's three chins wobbled. 'Computers or syn-thesisers or whatever. Here y'are.' She opened two cokes and pushed them across the counter. Smoke came out of the cans.

'Synthesisers have to be played too,' Meg told her. 'They don't play themselves y'know.'

'Ah.' Mabel put the pound note in the till and rummaged around for change. 'It's not the same. Give me a bit of Buddy Holly or Chuck Berry anytime. Here.' She counted coins into Sally's hand. 'Forty-six pence, four tens. And don't put that Meatloaf feller on – he scrambles your brains.'

They carried their drinks to a table near the juke-box. Sally fed the four tens into the slot, studied the selection and punched some buttons. The mechanism whirred and a thumping Meat-loaf intro blasted forth. The girls grinned across at Mabel, who threw her duster towards them, mouthed the word 'Monkeys' and disappeared into the back.

Sally stuck a straw into her can and sucked at it. The Meatloaf number ended and another began. Meg, her drink untouched, sat watching the coloured lights from the juke-box flashing on the grubby wall. After a while Sally said, 'Hey Meg – you're not drinking your coke. What's up?'

'Nothing.' Meg smiled faintly. 'I'm thinking, that's all.'

'What about? Not those daft exams I hope.'

She smiled again and shook her head. 'No.'

'What then – ghosts? Have you been seeing ghosts again Meg?'

Her tone was half mocking, half serious.

Meg nodded. 'Yes, but let's not talk about it, eh? We came here to enjoy ourselves.' She drank some coke and began drumming her fingers on the edge of the table in time with the music.

The record changed again. Meg drummed on. It began to get dark. The door opened and three boys came in. They recognised one from school. He recognised them too, and grinned and nodded at them. The other two were older. 'That one in the bomber jacket reminds me of John Travolta,' whispered Sally.

Len appeared, serving the boys with crisps and pop. They chose a table near the window and milled about, scraping chairs and laughing. One of them came towards the juke-box with a handful of coins. He didn't look at the two girls but said loudly, 'Don't reckon much to this rubbish someone's put on – let's have summat decent for a change.' He fed coins into the machine.

'Rubbish yourself,' muttered Sally. 'Just 'cause you think you're John Travolta.

'Sssh!' Meg frowned at her. 'He's trying to niggle us, Sal. Ignore him.'

The youth began pushing buttons. Without turning he called out, 'Hey, Len!'

'What's up?' Len had retrieved Mabel's cloth and was mopping the counter.

The boy hunched over the machine, stabbing out his selections. 'Somebody's left two babies over here.'

'Eh?' Len peered shortsightedly across the dim cafe. 'What you on about, lad?' The youth turned and pointed to Meg and Sally.

'These two. They look like they want feeding and changing to me.'

Len recognised the girls. 'What – Meg and Sally?' he said. 'They're all right. Sit down and leave them alone.'

The youth laid a hand on the back of Meg's chair. 'Yeah, well – me and my mates'd like to sit down,' he said, 'only these kids have got our table. I've just put a quidsworth of tens in this box and my mates can't hear the music.' He called to his companions. 'You can't hear the music, can you lads?'

The younger boy shook his head. 'Can't hear a thing,' he said.

'What music?' asked the other. The youth shrugged.

'There y'are old man – we're wasting good money, see? Now if you just tell these infants to shift, everything'll be all right, but if you don't . . .' He leaned over Meg's shoulder, picked up a heavy ashtray and hefted it, eyeing the glass shelving on the counter and the array of bottles behind Len's head.

'Hey, now just a minute . . .' Len started to come round the counter. Mabel's frightened face appeared in the doorway. At that moment the door opened and four boys in grubby overalls came in.

Meg, who had sat tense and fearful, cried out 'Paul!' and started to her feet.

Her brother took in the situation at a glance. He glared balefully at the youth with the ashtray. 'Put it down, Stebbins.'

'Sod off!' The youth turned slightly, threatening him.

Paul's lip curled. 'Throw that thing at me, Stebbins,' he grated, 'and I'll kick you to York and back.'

'You and whose army?'

Paul's three companions stood, fists clenched, at his shoulder. Their hands were roughened from heavy work, their faces streaked with dirt. 'Me and this army,' said Paul. 'You might as well give over, Stebbins, 'cause you're not fooling anybody. You've always been great at frightening little girls and pensioners but you're a muppet underneath.' He took a step forward. 'Drop the ashtray and get out, and take them with you.' He jerked his head towards the youth's friends, who sat watching the newcomers warily.

Stebbins hesitated, weighing his chances. For a moment it seemed to Meg that he would hurl the ashtray at Paul's head, but he didn't. Instead he shrugged and tossed it clattering on the table. 'Okay, Raven,' he said. 'We were leaving anyway. This dump's for kids but we'll be seeing you around, you can count on that. C'mon, Craig, Tony.' His friends joined him, and the three of them sidled past Paul and the others and left the café.

'Thanks, lads.' Len's relief showed in his face. 'I don't know what'd have happened if you hadn't come in.' He nodded towards the door. 'Yon's a nasty piece of work, Paul. D'you know him?'

Paul nodded. 'Oh yes, we know Stebbins all right. Don't we, lads?' The others grinned and nodded. 'We were at school with him, only he was a couple of years behind us. He'll still be there, in the fifth form, if he hasn't got himself chucked out. He's a right lossock and all – thinks he's hard 'cause he's nearly six foot, but he's soft as putty.'

'Aye, well.' Len was back behind the counter. 'You made him look daft just now, so I doubt if he'll show his face in here again. Come on – first order's on the house. Owt you fancy.'

Paul ignored his sister, sitting with his back to her at a table near the counter. Sally gazed across at the four boys. 'Weren't they great?' she said, dreamily. 'I wish I had a brother like Paul.'

'Huh!' Meg drained her can with a rude, gurgling noise. 'You wouldn't if you had to live with him. He's a pig. You should've seen his face when Mum and Dad were going on at me. Talk about the cat that got the cream.' Actually, at that moment, she couldn't help feeling thankful for her brother's existence: thankful and warm and a bit proud, even. In fact to her horror she felt like she had when she was small, when he'd come along and rescued her from some diminutive bully. She was determined not to show it though: not to Sally, and certainly not to Paul. She stood up.

'D'you want another coke?'

Sally nodded. 'Sure. But it was supposed to be my treat, remember?'

'I'm not broke, you know,' retorted Meg. 'I can buy you a coke if I want, can't I?'

Sally shrugged. 'Suit yourself.' She grinned wickedly. 'I reckon you're crazy about your brother really!'

Meg walked past the boys' table with her nose in the air. As she did so Paul said, 'If you're staying a while we might as well walk home together.'

She didn't look round, but tapped on the counter with a coin. 'Who wants to walk with you?' she sniffed. Mabel appeared and she said, 'Two cokes, please.'

'The Fitzroy Park strangler,' murmured Paul behind her. 'He's still loose y'know.'

'Thanks, Mabel.' She took her change and the two cans and brushed past her brother without bothering to reply.

Seventeen

At nine o'clock the place started to fill up. By half past all the tables were taken and those who had no seat stood around the juke-box. Meg and Sally were joined by two older girls whom they knew by sight but who ignored them. Sally fetched more cokes for herself and Meg. Len and Mabel were busy and the juke-box throbbed incessantly. It was dark outside.

Presently Sally looked at her watch and stifled a yawn. 'It's five past ten,' she said. 'I think I'd better be off. Coming?'

Meg shrugged. 'I'm supposed to be walking home with him.' She nodded at her brother's back. 'Stay and have one more coke, Sal. Then if he's not ready I'll come with you.'

Sally pulled a face and shook her head. 'Sorry, Meg. I'll have to go. Dad said ten, and anyway I'm shattered. You wait if you like.' She stood up.

Meg looked at her. 'Sure you don't mind, Sal?'

' 'Course not. It's only across the road. See you.' She turned, threading her way between crowded tables. A boy grabbed her chair and carried it off.

It was smoky. Meg wished Paul would hurry up. Her eyes stung and she didn't fancy another coke. The two girls talked across her as if she wasn't there. She slumped, half-asleep, gazing at the fuzzy coloured flashes on the wall.

When the record changed for perhaps the hundredth time she was vaguely aware that it was *Hangup*, by The Unwanted, belted out so that you heard the base through the soles of your feet. She let it go through her while the shifting lights kept time, combining with stains on the wall to make faces that came and went in purple, orange, green.

Faces. There came a stirring in her brain and somewhere low down unease flickered, like the very beginning of pain. A horizontal stain became a wing from beneath which six faces looked out, grinning. Indistinct voices droned through an anaesthesia of weariness and noise. *Hangup, hangup, hangup.* Numbness melted like smoke and she jerked erect with a cry, so that one of the girls stopped in mid-sentence and Paul twisted round in his seat.

'What's up?' The girl spoke sharply. Everybody was staring.

Meg shook her head. 'Sick,' she mumbled. 'I feel sick that's all.'

'Well don't be sick here,' snapped the girl. A chair scraped.

Paul bent, peering into her face. 'You all right, Meg?' She shook her head.

'No. I'm sick. Take me home please, Paul.'

'Okay.' He turned to his friends with a shrug and they mocked him, making the sort of noises puppies wring from people. 'Aaah!' they crooned. 'Aaah!'

He looked down at her and jerked his head towards the door. 'Come on.' His face was flushed and she knew he was furious with her. She got up, feeling her own cheeks burn. Paul barged across the café with his head down and Meg followed. Somebody laughed.

The night air was sharp after the warm fug. Paul strode away rapidly and Meg trotted in his wake, zipping her anorak. It was not until they were well clear of the café that he slowed down to let her catch up.

'What the heck was up with you back there?' he demanded. 'Why'd you make that stupid noise?' Meg shook her head.

'I don't know, Paul. I was so tired I started seeing things. It wasn't anything, really.'

'Well you made me look a right berk,' he said. 'I'm not your nanny, Meg. You want to stay away from the café if you can't keep out of trouble: I nearly got my head split open because of you!'

'It wasn't my fault.' She was close to tears. 'They wanted our table.'

'Huh!' Paul said no more but walked on with his head thrust forward and his hands in his pockets. Meg trailed miserably at his side and the voices echoed in her head. *Hangup, hangup, hangup* . . .

Eighteen

She dreamt she was cold – bitterly cold and her bones sang to an incessant vibration. Roaring filled her skull and she choked on an acrid stench. All around was darkness except the faint green luminescence from the instruments and the bright, criss-crossed pencils of probing light.

'*Hangup*!' The word repeated tinnily in her ears. 'We have a *hangup*, a *hangup*, a *hangup*.' She felt herself lifted, slammed down, lifted. Tilted this way, tilted that. Lighter than thistle-down, heavy as lead. 'No go, Skipper.' The tinny voice again. 'They're still with us.'

'Okay.' Another voice. A whine within the roar and a left-hand tilt, so steep her body stiffened fighting it – fighting the tilt towards falling.

'Look out, Baby – two o'clock!' Flashing lights. Smoke. An impact, and a scream that started in another throat and went on in her own.

Nineteen

When Meg came down to breakfast Paul and her parents were already seated round the table. She mumbled 'Good morning', slipped into her place and shook some cornflakes into her bowl, feeling their eyes on her. She'd woken them during the night and she knew it wouldn't be long before somebody mentioned it. She wished they wouldn't. She didn't know what to say. Whatever she said, Mum would probably go on about doctors, and this time Dad might agree with her. Paul would sit there smirking of course – especially after last night in the café. She poured milk on her cornflakes. Her father gave a little cough and she sighed. Here we go.

'All right this morning, Meg?'

She nodded. 'Yes thanks, Dad. Sorry I got you up.'

'That's all right, love – that's what dads are for.' He smiled wryly. 'I wish I knew what's worrying you, that's all. Something must be. Nobody has nightmares unless they're worried about something.'

'I think it's all imagination,' said her mother, as though Meg wasn't there. 'Her grandma keeps dropping hints about some gift she says Meg has – seeing things the rest of us don't see and that sort of nonsense.' She frowned. 'Perhaps she'd better stop going there at dinnertimes. They've both got over-ripe imaginations and they encourage each other.'

'It's stopping out late if you ask me,' said Paul maliciously. 'She nearly got me brained last night – I bet she was dreaming about that.'

'I was not!' retorted Meg. 'I wouldn't waste my time dreaming about you – and besides you can't be brained if you've got no brains, so there.'

'Nevertheless,' put in her father, 'you were late, Meg. I know you were with Paul, but twenty past ten is far too late for a girl of your age – I'm surprised he let you stay in that café so long. Anyway, it's not to happen again – d'you understand?'

Meg sighed. 'Yes, Dad.' Paul, nettled at having been included in the rebuke, stuck his tongue out at her.

As soon as she could, Meg slipped out of the house and headed for Fox Place. Last night's dream had left her puzzled as well as scared, and she hoped her grandmother might offer some explanation. At the very least the old lady would listen without getting angry or making fun of her.

When she turned the corner, Meg's heart sank. Four cars were parked in front of the cottage door. That meant that not only was her grandad in, but some of his cronies were there too. As she walked up the path she could see people in the front room. She lifted the brass knocker and rapped on the door.

'Oh – hello, Meg.' Henry Boyle, pipe in fist, smiled down at her. 'Come to see your grandma, have you?'

Meg nodded. 'If she's not too busy.'

'What?' The old man's grizzly eyebrows shot up. 'Your grandma – too busy to see you – now that'll be the day!' He ushered her inside. The room was crammed with people and blue with smoke. Most of the visitors were men, though two women occupied the settee. Meg was startled to recognise Dan Stamper among the men who were standing about, talking and smoking.

'We're having a bit of a meeting,' her grandad explained, steering her across the room. 'So I'm afraid you and your grandma will have to make do in here.' He led Meg through to the kitchen, where her grandmother was brewing tea in an enormous pot.

'I hope I'm not being a nuisance,' said Meg.

The old lady smiled. 'Not you, Meg.' She nodded towards the door. 'The nuisances are through there. Here.' She passed the great brown teapot to her husband. 'Take this through. I'll fetch the cups.'

She bustled about with sugar and biscuits and cups. When everything had been carried through, she closed the door and beamed at her grand-daughter.

'Now then, love – sit down and we'll have a cup ourselves.' She made tea, and Meg told her about her dream. 'What about hangup?' she asked when she had finished. 'Is it another nickname or something?' The old lady looked perplexed.

'No, Meg. It's not a nickname. It doesn't mean anything to me, and yet it seems you were meant to remember it. You say Baby was mentioned?'

Meg nodded. 'Yes. "Look out, Baby – it's two o'clock". Something like that.'

'Hmm. Tell you what.' Her grandmother got up. A pad and pencil hung on the side of a wall-cupboard. She scribbled on the top sheet and tore it off.

'There.' She sat down again. 'I've written it down, Meg. "Hangup", and "look out, Baby, it's two o'clock". I'll think about it, and if I come up with something I'll tell you on Monday. You are coming on Monday, aren't you?'

Meg nodded. 'Yes. Why?'

'Well – it's the holidays. I thought perhaps you'd have other plans.'

Meg shook her head. 'Mum'll still be writing her book. It's funny you should ask, though.' She told her grandma what her mother had said at breakfast. The old lady smiled sadly.

' "There are more things in heaven and earth",' she said.

'Eh?' Meg gaped at her.

'It's a quotation, Meg. Shakespeare. What I'm saying is, there's a great big chunk missing from your mum's life. She thinks if you can't see a thing, or hear it, or touch, smell or taste it, it doesn't exist, but she's wrong. That's why that novel of hers is no good.'

'Mum's book, no good?'

The old lady shook her head. ' 'Fraid not, Meg. Don't say anything, mind. When I say it's no good, I mean I don't think it'll ever be published. I wouldn't want her to stop writing it though.'

'Why not?' asked Meg, 'if she's wasting her time?'

'She's not wasting her time. It's nearly killing her. She slaves away at it, day after day, and yet when she reads through what she's done, it's not quite right. She can't put her finger on what's wrong, but I can – shall I tell you?'

Meg nodded.

'Imagination. What your mum would call overripe imagination. None of her characters has any. They behave like wooden puppets. This one does this, and that one says that, but none of them feels anything. They're chessmen, Meg, and one day, quite suddenly, your mum's going to tumble to what's missing, and then it won't be missing any more.' She smiled and added, 'I hope.'

Meg couldn't think of anything to say. A silence fell between them. They could hear the drone of voices in the front room. After a while Meg said, 'Who are those people, Grandma – what are they talking about?'

Her grandmother sighed. 'They're the Judy Woods Preservation Society, Meg. They're discussing what to do when work starts on the project tomorrow. Your grandad thinks I don't know what they're up to but I do. They mean to lie down in front of the lorries.'

'Really?' Meg's eyes lit up momentarily, then she frowned. 'Why do they want to stop it, Grandma – why can't they see it's a good thing?'

The old lady shook her head. 'Things affect people different ways, Meg. What's good for some may not be good for others. I hope nobody gets hurt, that's all.'

Twenty

By eight o'clock that Monday morning, Meg and Sally were in the field beside the wood. They were not alone. Word had got round that the Judy Woods Preservation Society meant to stage its most determined protest to date, and half the village had turned out to see the fun.

The work was due to commence at half-past eight. At ten past the spectators, who had been standing around gossiping and cracking jokes, heard marching feet along the road. Somebody called out 'Here they come!' and everybody looked towards the gateway. Henry Boyle appeared, carrying a placard and flanked by two men. They wheeled smartly in between the granite gateposts with the members of the Society behind them. As they advanced along the footpath they began to chant:

> 'Judy Woods is here to stay –
> Townhall vandals keep away!'

An ironic cheer greeted this chant, and the marchers repeated it over and over as they drew near. The spectators moved off the footpath to let them through. When Henry reached the entrance to the wood he turned. The marchers broke ranks and gathered round him. There were about seventy of them.

Nodding and smiling to the spectators, old Henry held up his hands for silence and began to speak.

'Fellow villagers,' he began. 'We are here this morning to show the authorities that Wilberforce doesn't want this so-called nature park and leisure reserve. This magnificent turn-out is all the proof we need that the village is one hundred percent against the scheme and has been from the start.'

'Hoy!' cried a voice in the crowd. 'Don't include us, you old crackpot – we're only here for the beer.' Laughter greeted this remark and Meg felt her face go red. Henry Boyle continued as though he hadn't heard.

'Over the last few days,' he said, 'we have made vigorous representations to the authorities on behalf of the village . . .'

'On behalf of who?' somebody yelled, and the old man repeated, 'On behalf of the village, but we have been ignored, so we are left with no alternative than to take direct action.'

His supporters began to cheer loudly and he held up his hands again. 'This is not the time for cheering,' he told them. 'There'll be time for that when we've won and in the meantime, let's get organised.' He stuck his placard into the soft earth. His followers began lying down in the gateway. Old Henry went from one to another, arranging them into an impassable barrier while cries of 'Shame!' and 'Loonies!' rose from the crowd.

There was a sound of motors and a jeep appeared with four men in it. This was followed by an earth-mover and two open trucks full of youths. Henry Boyle moved to meet the jeep. It stopped and a man in a suit got out, looking angry. He glared at the old man and said, 'Are you responsible for those people?'

Henry nodded. 'They're the Judy Woods Preservation Society, and I'm their Secretary.'

'We're not all with him,' called a voice from the crowd. 'Only those lying down.'

'Run over 'em!' cried somebody else. The man looked at Henry.

'Get them out of the way,' he said. 'We've got a job to do.'

Henry shook his head. 'Not here you haven't. We don't want you, so you can just take yourselves back where you came from.'

The man sighed. 'Look,' he said, 'you'll save yourselves and us a lot of trouble if you'll just tell 'em to get up and go home.'

'They're not budging,' growled Henry Boyle. The man turned and said something to the driver. The jeep's engine roared and it began crawling towards a woman in a blue anorak who lay across the path.

'Get up, you silly cow!' somebody shouted. The woman

didn't move. The vehicle rolled towards her. When only inches separated the wheels and her body the driver braked and began sounding his horn. The woman stared up at the sky without blinking.

The driver got out and the two men walked back to where the earth-mover had pulled up. The truck drivers got down from their cabs and the men went into a huddle, talking quietly. The boys in the trucks began to sing 'Why are we waiting?' Some of the spectators joined in.

Presently the man in the suit came back. The singing tailed off. 'Mr Boyle,' he said, 'if your people aren't off this field in five minutes we shall call the police.'

'Go on then,' Henry replied. 'There's only the one constable in Wilberforce so you'll have to fetch 'em from York, and when they get here they'll have to drag us away one by one.'

'We'll drag 'em away!' shouted a spectator, and there were noises of assent. The man shook his head.

'No. Take the law into your own hands and you'll find yourselves up for assault.' He spoke to the driver of the jeep, who roared off the way he had come. Henry Boyle glowered at the man and went to lie among his friends.

'Oh Sal,' whispered Meg. 'I hope they won't hurt Grandad. I know he's stubborn but he's only doing what he thinks is right.'

Sally smiled and squeezed her arm. 'They won't hurt him, Meg. I've seen 'em on telly – they just lift 'em out of the way.'

A few of the spectators drifted off, preferring not to stay now that the police were involved. Everything went quiet. The drivers leaned against one of the trucks, smoking. The spectators shuffled their feet and looked towards the road. In the trucks, the boys whispered together. The protestors lay with their eyes closed or stared into the sky, listening. The sun climbed, evaporating the dew so that a faint mist dimmed the distant hedges.

Presently a siren was heard. People stirred. A driver threw down his cigarette-butt and ground it out with his heel. The protestors grew tense. Meg caught her bottom lip between her teeth and felt for Sally's hand.

The siren grew louder. A white car turned on to the field

and came jolting across the grass, followed by two vans. They pulled up close to the trucks. An inspector got out of the car and spoke to the man in the suit. The two of them came over to the protestors.

'I have to warn you,' said the inspector, 'that by lying here you are all committing an offence. However, if you remove yourselves at once no action will be taken against you. If you do not, my men will be forced to physically remove you and in that case you may be charged with obstruction. You have two minutes.'

The protestors didn't respond. The inspector stood with his hands clasped behind him, rocking on his heels and gazing into the sky. After a time he glanced at his wristwatch and said, 'Ten seconds.' Nobody stirred. The seconds ticked away.

'Right!' The inspector spun on his heel and rapped out an order. The van doors opened and policemen poured out. Without speaking they went among the protestors and began lifting them away from the footpath. There was no resistance. They hung like sacks of potatoes till they were put down, then sat and watched the same thing happening to their friends.

The council drivers started their engines and rolled forward. The first truck knocked down Henry's placard, the second ground it into the mud and the earth-mover ripped it to splinters as the spectators cheered and began to disperse.

Twenty-One

By the time the workforce broke four days later for the Easter weekend, Judy Woods had undergone a transformation. Teams of boys had scoured the length and breadth of the wood, picking up rubbish which had been accumulating since before they were born. They found armchairs and mattresses, fridges and washing-machines, cars and prams and mouldering mounds of rags.

They worked their way along the stream, throwing out tins and toys and twisted bits of steel. All this stuff was loaded on lorries and carted off to the disused quarry the council used as a dump. Each morning Meg and Sally turned up to watch, and so did most of their friends. Every evening, Paul came home dirty and furious, muttering about the filthy stuff he'd had to touch that day and every dinnertime, Meg and her grandma had a good old moan together – Meg about her dream, and the old lady about her husband's forthcoming court appearance for obstruction.

When work resumed after the four-day break, trucks came with bricks, sections of pipe and loads of sand and gravel. Trenches were dug, concrete mixed and poured, pipes laid. One trench ran out of the wood and across the field to the road. Paul began learning to drive the earth-mover, which improved his mood. Once, Radar and some of his friends appeared They sat astride their stuttering machines for a while, not saying anything, then roared off, throwing up clods of clay.

The holidays slipped by as holidays will, and long before they were ready, the village children returned to school. Meg was tired. She had been absorbed watching the work in the wood, but her sleep now was broken nightly by the same dream. She hung freezing in the night-sky while a voice in her ear screamed '*Hangup, hangup, hangup.*'

Twenty-Two

April gave way to May. Drifts of bluebells appeared under the trees and filled the warm air with their cloying scent. The tender green that swathed the wood left no trace of the squalor which had reigned there for so long.

On the building site, work was well advanced. The neat, brick-built café and toilet blocks were being faced with slabs of honey-coloured stone and a team of boys was busy putting in windows under the critical eye of a glazier.

Paul and his team were improving the footpath – filling in ruts and potholes and shoring up the edge in places where it had started to crumble down on to the slope. Only Boggy Hollow, with its marshy ground and tight-packed alders, remained untouched.

Most people had got fed-up with watching the work by now, and when Meg and Sally arrived by way of the playing-field that Friday afternoon before the May holiday, they were the only spectators except for a girl called Tracey Sugden, whose father was one of the supervisors.

'Wow!' exclaimed Sally, as they looked down on to the patched and levelled footpath. 'It's really coming along now, isn't it?'

Meg nodded. 'Be finished soon, I expect.'

'Will it heck!' scoffed Tracey Sugden, who was inclined to be rude.

The friends glared at her. 'Who rattled your cage, Sugden?' demanded Meg.

'My dad's a supervisor,' the girl replied, 'and he says the biggest job's not started yet.' She looked smug. They waited, but she offered no further information and after a minute Sally said, 'What job's that, then?'

'Boggy Hollow.'

Meg looked at her. 'What are they going to do with it – drain all the water out?'

'No, stupid. It's got rare plants in it, and a rare sort of spider called the raft-spider. They're going to put a path through the middle so people can go in and have a look.'

'Ugh!' cried Sally. 'Who the heck wants to see spiders?'

'And how d'you put a path in a bog?' said Meg. 'It'll sink.'

The girl shrugged. 'I don't know, but they are. My dad says so, and he's . . .'

'A supervisor!' mocked the others in unison. The girl shot them a venomous glance, tossed her head and stalked off.

Meg and Sally walked along to the site and spent a few minutes watching the boys fixing windows. It was possible now to imagine what the area would be like when it was finished. There would be picnic tables under the trees, and a concrete pad with a slide, a roundabout and a couple of other rides for the smaller kids. A patch of ground had already been cleared and levelled for this.

At four o'clock the two girls set off home. They parted at the bottom of Newside Road, having agreed to meet there at nine next morning.

At half-past five Paul came home looking pleased with himself. 'I handled the earth-mover by myself today,' he announced.

'Good lad,' approved his father. 'How was it?'

'Easy.'

'Sally and I were there after school,' Meg told him, 'but we didn't see you.'

Her brother shook his head. 'You wouldn't. We were right on by Boggy Hollow, but this morning I cleared a square for the playground. It's next to the café.'

Meg nodded. 'We saw it. Tracey Sugden says there's going to be a path through Boggy Hollow – is there?'

Paul nodded. 'Yes. We start it on Tuesday. That's why some of us were there this afternoon, having a look.'

'How will you manage?' asked Mrs Raven. 'Won't it sink or something?'

'That's what I said,' put in Meg.

Paul shook his head. 'They build roads across all sorts of marshy places, don't they? What you do is, you tip rubble in – tons and tons of it, till it's above the level of the bog. Then it's rolled flat and you lay a surface on it – tarmac or concrete. I've been promised a crack at the roller, too.'

Mr Raven frowned. 'The far side of that hollow's on Dan Stamper's land, isn't it?'

Paul nodded. 'Yes. And the miserable old skinflint wasn't going to sell – said he didn't want millions of sightseers traipsing across his land, but the council made him sell a bit. Just enough to take the path round the edge of the bog and back to the footpath. He was so mad he joined old Henry's group!'

His father nodded. 'That's right. There was a bit in the Star about it.'

Paul went out after tea. Mr Raven tinkered with the car till it started to get dark, then went off to his club. Meg was watching T.V. but as soon as the two of them were alone, her mother started going on about how tired Meg looked, and how she wished she'd agree to see a doctor instead of talking to her grandma. Meg told her she didn't understand, and this made her angry, and by half-past nine Meg was in her room, dabbing her cheeks with a damp tissue and looking at her pink eyes in the dressing-table mirror.

'She thinks I'm going queer in the head,' she sniffled to her reflection. She blew her nose, dropped the tissue in the bin and started to get ready for bed. Her throat ached and she could hardly keep her eyes open, but she knew it would be ages before she slept. She would lie fighting sleep because of the dream, and then when she did drop off the dream would wake her and she'd lie there for hours, terrified in case the blind man came again. She longed for it all to stop, knowing that if it didn't she'd have to give in and let her mother take her to the doctor.

She switched on her tiny radio, turned out the light and got into bed. Dad hadn't got round to fixing the bedside lamp yet, and she'd taken to having the radio on for company. It was tuned to an all-night station. The voices of the disc-jockeys made her feel less afraid, and with the volume low she sometimes listened till one or two in the morning. Once or twice she'd fallen asleep with it on, and woken from her nightmare to find its soothing murmur in her ear.

She lay down, closed her eyes and let the music wash over her. It wasn't too bad early on, with Mum downstairs and ordinary sounds outside. She fancied she could feel the tension draining out of her, like in an ad for headache pills. The disc-jockey burbled cheerfully and tune followed tune. A delicious warmth spread through Meg's body. She dozed.

Exactly when the radio started to go wrong, she never knew. She'd been asleep, and woke to hear voices coming out of the set. Her first thought was that the station must be transmitting a play, though she knew it never did. Then as she came wider awake she discerned something chillingly familiar about these disembodied voices. She lay rigid as the words spilled tinnily into the dark room.

'. . . York . . . I tell you we're too far north . . . shape of the river – unmistakable, even in this stuff. . . . south, skipper . . . south.'

A crackle of static, then '. . . sorry, they must've . . . compass.' More static, with a voice behind it. Meg strained her ears.

'. . . bloody York again . . . one-eight-o . . . starboard, skipper – starboard for chrissake now!' A click, then '. . . can't hold her – . . . tight everybody . . . going in . . .'

The brief silence that followed was broken by the smooth pseudo-American voice of the disc-jockey who said, 'And so now, specially for you, Dawn, way down there in Chatham, here's the Unwanted with their latest hit single, *Hangup*.'

Twenty-Three

As soon as she'd finished breakfast, Meg hurried round to her grandma's. She had to talk to her but if she was quick, she might still be able to meet Sally at nine o'clock. When she got there, her grandad had already gone to his allotment. The old lady took one look at Meg's face and made her sit down in an armchair.

'Whatever's happened, Meg?' she asked. 'You look absolutely wild – like a prophet who's seen a vision or something and come rushing in straight from the desert to tell everybody about it!'

'Better than that, Grandma!' cried Meg. 'I think I've got the answer.'

'The answer to what, dear?'

'The answer to my ghosts. I heard Grandad and the others on my radio last night.'

'You . . .' Her grandmother, mouth open, lowered herself into the other armchair. 'What on earth do you mean, Meg?'

'I had the radio on, it was late, and suddenly the music wasn't there and there were these voices – the same ones as in my dream. Quacky voices, like they were talking through mikes. One of them mentioned York. He said he could see the river, and they were too far north.' She looked into her grandmother's eyes. 'Where was Grandad's base, Grandma?'

The old lady lowered her eyes and sat staring into the empty hearth for a while without speaking. 'Church Fentham,' she murmured at last. 'He was stationed just a few miles down the road at Church Fentham. That's why I came to live here.'

Meg shot forward in her chair. 'Yes, and Church Fentham's south of here, isn't it? If a plane was making for Church Fentham and it flew over York it'd be too far north, wouldn't it?'

Her grandmother gazed at her blankly. 'Why yes, Meg – I suppose it would. But . . .'

'Don't you see!' Meg's eyes shone. 'Grandad's plane was over York. One of the men -- somebody called him Skip – said "We're going in." That means crashing, 'cause I've heard it on the telly. That bomber came down somewhere nearby, Grandma: *that's* what they've been trying to tell me all this time!'

'No, Meg.' The old lady shook her head. 'I'm sorry dear but that's impossible – quite impossible. Michael's plane was seen, trailing smoke and losing height off Heligoland. They'd been to Kiel, and on the way back his plane started to fall behind. It must have been damaged in some way – the others couldn't get it on the radio – and it fell behind. It was dawn. An enemy fighter appeared and attacked it. They always went for the stragglers. The last anybody saw of it, the bomber was going down with smoke pouring from an engine, so you see . . .' She smiled sadly. 'It couldn't possibly have got back, Meg. Heligoland is hundreds of miles away.'

'But Grandma . . .' Meg's eyes brimmed with tears. 'Why would they – why would I get to hear all that stuff on my radio if it didn't mean anything?'

Her grandmother shook her head. 'I don't know, dear.' She reached for Meg's hands and squeezed them. 'Strange things happen on the airwaves. I read an article where somebody picked up part of a speech broadcast twenty years earlier by Winston Churchill, and people have found themselves listening to the voices of broadcasters who have been dead years. As I told you once before, Meg – there are more things in heaven and earth . . .'

'I know.' Meg swallowed hard to keep from crying. 'But I still think this radio thing's part of the message, else why did they play *Hangup* straight after?'

The old lady shrugged. 'Coincidence, Meg. Even I can't believe they've got a disc-jockey working for them. And I've thought and thought about hangup and it still means nothing to me.'

'It's part of the message,' Meg insisted. 'It keeps cropping up. It was on the juke-box that night in the café. It's in my dreams, and now it comes over the radio. And I *know* it was Grandad's plane over York – I just know.'

Her grandmother sighed. 'I've tried to explain how impossible that is, dear. I am sorry.'

'Yes, well . . .' Meg stood up. 'I've got to go. I'm supposed to be meeting Sal. Oh . . .' She unzipped her shoulder bag and fished out a roll of papers with a rubber-band round them. 'I nearly forgot. Mum asked me to give you this. It's the latest chapter. 'Bye.'

The old lady followed her to the door and called after her. 'I really am sorry I can't agree about York, Meg. Do let me know if anything else happens, won't you?'

'Sure.' She was hurt and disappointed but she turned and forced a smile before walking rapidly away in the warm sunshine.

When she reached the bottom of Newside Road it was nearly twenty-past nine and there was no sign of Sally. Meg hung about for a minute or two, then called at the house.

'She left nearly half an hour ago, Meg,' Mrs Barnet told her. 'I thought she was meeting you.'

Meg thanked her and went down to the corner. Sally was probably in the woods. There'd be nothing happening, this being Saturday, but some of the kids might be mooching about. She turned left and walked along past the school.

It had rained in the night and the earth between the granite posts, churned up by the wheels of heavy vehicles, was a morass. Meg had trainers on, and had to teeter from ridge to sticky ridge between troughs of clayey water. She didn't look up till she reached a dryish bit of footpath and when she did, she saw that a police-car was parked near the gateway at the far end. 'Oh-oh!' she muttered, 'I wonder what's up this time?'

As she approached the car two uniformed officers came out of the woods. Between them, talking heatedly and waving his arms about, came Dan Stamper. When he spotted Meg he pointed and said, 'See – here's a friend of his, come to laugh I expect. I seen 'er with 'im one time.'

The unexpectedness of the encounter stopped Meg in her tracks, and before she could gather her wits one of the officers, a woman, called out, 'Just a minute, love – we'd like a word with you.'

Meg approached the trio with trepidation. What was the old devil talking about – had it something to do with the bike-boys or what? She stood in front of them on jelly legs and said, 'Yes?'

'This gentleman says you're friendly with a boy called Craig Darke. Are you?'

Meg shook her head.

'No. I don't know anybody called that.'

'Not much, you don't!' sneered Stamper. 'I seen you with 'im only t'other week – 'im in 'is fancy red 'elmet!'

'Oh.' Meg felt her cheeks redden. 'You mean Radar. I didn't know his real name, and you never saw me with him either.'

'But you talk to him sometimes?' countered the woman.

'Only once,' said Meg. 'I was here with my friend. These lads came on bikes and Radar spoke to me. I only know he's called Radar 'cause it's on his helmet.'

'What did – Radar talk to you about?'

'Oh – I told him about the nature park. He didn't know.'

'And when you told him, what did he say?'

Meg shook her head. 'I don't remember. He was a bit mad I think. They used to ride here, you see.'

'There y'are!' cried Stamper. 'What did I tell you?'

The woman ignored him. 'What's your name, love?'

'Meg Raven.'

'Address?'

'Nineteen Nearside Avenue.'

'And you never saw Craig Darke before that day?'

'No.'

'But you saw him again, didn't you – the night you bumped into this gentleman. I think you saw him commit an offence, didn't you?'

Meg hesitated. She had nothing against Radar, but on the other hand she had no idea what this was all about, and if he'd done something serious she didn't want to get mixed up as an accessory or anything. She nodded, biting her lip.

'Yes. I saw him knock some posts over and drag some tape around. Him and some others. I hid till they'd gone.'

'And you didn't think of telling the police?'

She nodded. 'I thought of it, yes. But it didn't seem like anything very bad, and I didn't want to get him into trouble.'

'Ah!' The policewoman shook her head. 'You should have reported him, Meg. If you had, you might have saved him more serious trouble.'

'What d'you mean?' asked Meg. 'Has he . . .'

'Never you mind. You can go now, only think on – if you see an offence, tell the police. It's your duty.'

They went towards the car. Meg walked on. Her legs were wobbly and she felt sick. She picked her squelchy way through into the wood, and a scene of destruction met her gaze.

Every pane of glass in the café was smashed. The small, glass-brick windows of the toilet block were starred and pitted from heavy blows and the two freshly-painted doors hung crookedly from burst hinges. Facing-stones had been wrenched away and smashed on the concrete path. Somebody had used a red spray-can to scrawl 'York aggro' in huge letters on the café wall.

Meg groaned softly. There was a tinkling of glass and Sally appeared from behind the toilets. 'This is nothing,' she called. 'Come and look in here.' She pushed one of the ruined doors aside. Meg ran over and looked in.

All the hand-basins had been ripped out of the wall and reduced to a heap of fragments on the floor. Twisted copper piping and chunks of plaster lay scattered about. Cubicle doors had been kicked in. There was water everywhere.

'It's the same with the café,' Sally told her. 'They've pulled the sink out and flooded the place, and there's broken glass and wiring all over the floor.'

'I thought there was a watchman here at night,' said Meg.

Sally shrugged. 'He'd be at the pub. Dad's seen him there a few times.'

Meg nodded. 'Didn't the police see you?'

Sally shook her head. 'No. I got down behind a bush when I heard the car. Desperate Dan was with them. He must have found it like this and called them. Did they say anything to you?'

'Yes.' She told Sally what had happened.

When she had finished Sally said, 'So it was Radar and his gang. I never would have thought it, Meg.' Meg shrugged.

'I told you they were vandals, didn't I?'

Sally pulled a face. 'What'll happen to him, d'you think?'

'He'll get arrested,' said Meg. 'They're probably arresting him right now. They'll take him to court, and he'll be sent to prison.'

'He's not old enough!'

'Borstal then, and it'll serve him right.' She touched a chunk of porcelain with her toe. 'All that work for nothing.'

'Hey, come on, Meg!' Sally grinned. 'They'll make it just as nice again, you'll see – let's pick some bluebells.'

Meg felt a twinge of envy. Nothing ever worried Sal for long.

She forced a smile. 'Okay.' They walked out into the sunshine.

Twenty-Four

If the wreckers had hoped their action would hold up progress on the project, they were to be disappointed. That same afternoon, Paul got a phone call. Some of the workers had volunteered to give up their May holiday to repair the damage. Was Paul prepared to join them?

Paul was, and throughout Sunday and Monday the site was a hive of determined industry. Villagers who turned up to watch found themselves pressed into service as moppers-up. Fresh supplies of piping, plaster, glass and utensils were rushed from the city. Plumbers, plasterers and glaziers worked flat out with the boys and by dusk on Monday, the place was almost restored to its state of near-completion.

'There y'are!' crowed Sally, as the two girls walked home through the twilight. 'I told you they'd make it nice again, didn't I?' And Meg, who was thinking about something else entirely, nodded.

Meg was brooding about the voices she'd heard on her radio. It had nagged at her all weekend. She felt sure she was right – her grandad's bomber had made it back to York. Her grandmother's dismissal of the idea had left her in a quandary. Who could she turn to now? Who was there, who knew about the war and would support her? It was not until she was in bed that night that she thought of Mr Leacock.

Mr Leacock taught maths and science and knew all about computers, but his hobby was aeroplanes and the Second World War. He collected models and photographs and all sorts of odds and ends, and he sometimes dug bits of crashed aeroplanes out of the ground. If anybody round here was an expert on that sort of thing, it was Mr Leacock.

She'd have to be careful what she said to him, though. He wasn't the sort of man who believed in ghosts and dreams. If she started telling him all that stuff he'd think she was barmy and send her packing. She wanted to ask him whether she might be right about Grandad's bomber, but she wouldn't call it Grandad's bomber and she'd need a reason for asking. She lay thinking, and at last she had it.

'Of course!' she whispered. 'Mum's book. Old Leacock knows Mum writes. I'll say she wants to know for her book.'

She caught him in the corridor at morning break. He was striding towards the staffroom and his coffee, and she had to run after him.

'Excuse me, Mr Leacock!'

He stopped and turned. 'Yes, Meg – what is it?'

'It's about the war, Sir, and bombers. Can I ask you something, only my mum wants to know for her book?'

He grinned. 'Ask away, only make it snappy. My coffee's going cold.'

'Yes Sir. Could a bomber get back from Heligoland if it was smoking, Sir?'

'Oh, yes. Depending on how badly it was damaged of course. They had four engines and often limped home on three.'

'Yes, Sir. And could a bomber get back to England and then crash, and nobody ever find it?'

'Hmm.' Mr Leacock looked doubtful. 'Tell your Mum that's a bit of a long shot, Meg. You see, normally they'd be in radio contact with their base, so if they crashed the base would know approximately where they'd come down and the wreck would be found.'

'But if the radio wasn't working?' persisted Meg.

The teacher shrugged. 'In that case yes, possibly. If the aircraft came down in a lake or river, or in some very remote spot. The Scottish Highlands, perhaps.' He grinned again. 'D'you think I might have my coffee now?'

'Oh, yes. Sorry, Sir. And thanks – my mum'll be very grateful.' She went out through the cloakroom, deep in thought.

'It is possible then,' she muttered to herself. 'Just possible that Grandma's wrong and I'm right.' It didn't prove anything of course, but it would have to do for now.

Twenty-Five

At teatime on Wednesday Paul said, 'It's great working in Boggy Hollow. That earth-mover goes through mud as if it wasn't there, and you should see the trees fall in front of it.' He made engine-noises and waved his arms about to show them what it was like.

'Have you cleared a way right through?' his father asked.

Paul shook his head. 'We're nearly halfway. What we do is we go in, knock some trees over, scoop 'em up with the bucket, reverse out and drop 'em in a pile. Then a tipper backs up and dumps a load of filler, the roller rolls it flat and then we go in and knock the next lot of trees down. There's scrap iron in there as well. We got some out today and there's loads more just ahead. We make a separate pile of that.'

Mr Raven frowned. 'Scrap iron? How on earth did that get there?'

Paul pulled a face. 'Dunno.'

Meg, who had been making fork-patterns in her mashed potato and only half listening, felt her heart quicken. She looked up and said, 'What's it like, Paul?'

'Ice-cream,' said her brother, sarcastically. 'Chocolate ice-cream with crushed nuts.'

'Paul!' Mrs Raven shot him a reproving glance. 'It was a perfectly sensible question. Answer it sensibly, please.'

Paul shrugged. 'It's just iron. Twisted sheets of rusty iron. I suppose they dumped old cars there at one time.'

Mr Raven shook his head. 'Not very likely, lad,' he said. 'How would they have got 'em through the trees, eh? Not to mention the mud.'

Paul shrugged again. 'I don't know. That's what it looks like, that's all. It doesn't really matter, does it?'

It mattered to Meg. She said no more, but when the meal was over and her brother went upstairs, she followed him.

'Paul?'

He paused on the landing. 'What?'

'That iron. Is it anything like an aeroplane?'

He laughed. 'What sort of daft question's that?'

'No, seriously, Paul – is it?'

'Is it heck!' He started going into his room.

'Wait!'

He turned with a sigh. 'Look Meg,' he said. 'I'm going out and I've got to get ready, right? I don't know what you're on about and I don't want to know, so go away and leave me alone.'

'I'm on about Grandad's bomber.'

'I might have known.' He rested his hand on the doorframe and his forehead on the hand. 'Look,' he said quietly, 'you know what Mum's always telling you about that stuff. You're barmy, Meg, and if you don't cut it out they'll come and take you away.' He turned to look at her and she was surprised to see real concern in his eyes. 'And I wouldn't want that, even if you are a pain in the neck.' He gazed at her for a moment as her eyes filled with tears, then went into his room and closed the door.

Twenty-Six

In the middle of the night the wind rose, drawing a black curtain of cloud across the sky. It swooped, booming and racketing about the house, rattling window-frames and spattering the panes with squally rain.

The small top window in Meg's room lifted with every gust then dropped, its worn catch slamming on the peg. The wardrobe door swung open to reveal pale garments, hanging.

In the bed, Meg stirred and woke. She had dreamt, and the storm – noise and the cold were like the dream, so that for a time she did not know she was awake. A faint green luminescence lit the face that gazed with anxious eyes into her own while beyond, in the twitch and ripple of the curtain, other faces formed.

A sudden waft blew sleep away like cloud from the face of the moon. Sick with horror she shrank away – shrank from things that walk with equal ease in dreams and on the earth – things that walked and watched her when they should be in their graves.

And then, with the first faint roll of thunder they were gone, and there was only the curtain and the clock and the beating of her heart.

And the wardrobe, with her dresses on their hangers there inside. She stared dully across the room and counted the dresses, chanting their message in her head. *One, two, three. Hangup, hangup, hangup.*

Twenty-Seven

When Mr Leacock got to school at twenty-past eight that Thursday morning, Meg was there already. She had been in the entrance hall since eight, watching the gateway for his green Citroen. As he pushed through the swing-doors she intercepted him.

'Mr Leacock?'

'Meg – what on earth are you doing here at this time of the morning?'

'I've got to ask you something, sir.'

'What – now? Couldn't it have waited till breaktime?'

Meg shook her head. 'No, sir. I – I think it's important.'

'Well, all right then.' He tucked his briefcase under his arm, the better to look at his watch. 'Let's make it a quickie though – I've a lesson to prepare.'

She nodded. 'I'll be quick, sir. What does hangup mean?'

'Hangup?' He frowned. 'It's an American expression, isn't it? It means something that's a problem in your life – like if you hate to travel in lifts, they say you've got a hangup about lifts.'

'No, sir.' Meg shook her head. 'I don't mean that. I mean, if you were in a bomber in the war, what would hangup mean then?'

The teacher looked at her. 'Meg,' he said, perplexed. 'Your mum wouldn't send you along at this time of day to gather information for a book, so come on – what's this really all about, eh?'

Meg looked at the floor. 'I don't know, sir. I can't explain. I've got to know, that's all.'

'Yes, and you seem pretty desperate about it too, young woman.' Gently, he lifted her chin with his fingertips so that she had to meet his gaze. 'You do know that if you're ever in any sort of trouble, you can come to your teachers and they'll understand and try to help, don't you, Meg?'

She nodded, an aching lump in her throat. 'Yes, thank you, sir. I'm not in trouble, honestly. I just have to know what hangup means.'

He sighed and shook his head. 'You're a strange one, Meg Raven, and no mistake. Still . . .' He shrugged. 'If you've got to know, you've got to know. A hangup was when a plane couldn't get rid of its bombs – when the release-mechanism failed.'

Meg's heart gave a kick and her eyes widened. 'What happened then?'

'Well – the pilot might throw the plane about a bit – try to shake 'em loose.'

'And if that didn't work?'

The teacher made a wry face. 'Then they'd have to bring their bombs home. It happened a lot.'

Meg said nothing but stood, chewing her lip while her mind raced. So hangup did mean something. It did. But why should it keep coming into her nightmares? What was so . . .

When the answer hit her, it was all she could do to keep from crying out. Her face grew pale and she whispered, 'What if they crashed – what would happen then?'

The teacher shrugged again. 'Usually, the whole thing would go up – plane, bombs, fuel – the whole issue. But sometimes it didn't. Sometimes there'd be no explosion, and then the bomb-disposal boys would have to come along and make the bombload safe.'

'But what if they couldn't find it?' pursued Meg. 'If nobody knew where it was?' The suspicion in her mind was solidifying into a horrible certainty.

'Then it would lie there for ever, Meg. Till it rotted I mean.' He smiled. 'Can I go and prepare that lesson now?'

'Sir?' She looked so odd and spoke so urgently that he paused; little lines of impatience appeared at the corners of his mouth. 'Sir,' she said in a small, dry voice. 'There's a bomber in Boggy Hollow with bombs in it, and those boys are going to try to move it today and one of them's my brother.'

Twenty-Eight

Mr Leacock stood looking at her. She wanted to grab his arm and drag him outside but she knew that if she did, he'd think she was hysterical. He'd summon other members of staff and they'd take her to the first-aid room and hold her down while the Head phoned her mother. And in the meantime, out at Boggy Hollow, Paul would be banging away with his earth-mover. Banging away . . .

After what seemed to her a long time he said, 'How do you know this, Meg?' She hesitated. How could she answer without making him think she was insane?

'I – you won't believe me, sir,' she stammered, trying to keep her voice level. 'I've been having dreams about it. Nightmares.' She decided not to mention the ghosts. 'I don't expect you to believe me. I didn't believe it myself, but then yesterday my brother told me he dredged up some pieces of aeroplane, and it all seemed to fit.'

As she spoke she watched his face, hoping her embroidery of the truth might capture his interest. He dropped his briefcase into one of the airmchairs provided for visitors and put his hands in his pockets.

'You know, Meg, this is pretty fantastic,' he said. 'I mean, it's so damned unlikely, even if you weren't basing it all on dreams you've had. Boggy Hollow's no great size. If there is a plane in there – a bomber – why wasn't it found years ago?'

'I don't know, Mr Leacock. Nobody ever goes in there.' She fought back tears. 'All I know is, people are going to get blown up if we don't do something. Come with me sir – please. It'll only take a few minutes and if I'm lying, you can punish me and I'll deserve it. Please, sir!'

He glanced at his watch, then through the glass doors. A car was turning into the driveway, manoeuvring between knots of dawdling children in the early sunshine. School would not start for half an hour yet.

'All right, Meg,' he said. 'I'll come, but I warn you: if this turns out to be some kind of hoax on your part you'll be sorry – very sorry indeed.'

She shot him a grateful glance and turned, barging through the swingdoors and running along the path that skirted the building. Leacock followed. Curious eyes watched till the pair passed from sight round the side of the school.

'This way, sir!' Meg swerved, sprinting out across the playing-field and scrambling over the fence.

'Hey, steady on!' gasped Leacock behind her. 'I'm not used to this.'

She waited till he'd cleared the fence, then ran on into the wood. They pelted down through the trees to the footpath and turned left.

'It's – just on here, sir.' They were approaching the wide bend before Boggy Hollow. Meg's lungs burned and her legs felt leaden, but she had a picture in her head of the earth-mover with her brother at the controls and something in its bucket that smoked and ticked.

They came off the bend and Meg looked down to her left. Below her a new pathway of crushed rubble bisected the marshy ground across which she had fled from the sightless watcher, and led between stumps of smashed alders down into the Hollow. Somewhere at the end of that pathway, invisible to her because of the trees, was Paul on his great machine. Two vehicles were visible – a truck and a road-roller – and figures in donkey-jackets and wellingtons were moving about on the pathway with shovels and rakes and wheelbarrows. To one side she saw a stack of felled trees, like an enormous bonfire waiting to be lit and beside it, a smaller stack of metal. She waited till the teacher caught up with her, then pointed to the heaped metal, praying he might recognise something.

He stood, breathing hard and following the direction of her finger. 'No good,' he panted, 'from here. Have to get closer.' She could tell by his voice that he regretted having come.

Reluctantly, he began to pick his way down the muddy slope. Meg followed, wishing she could make him hurry. She fancied she could hear the earth-mover crunching towards its doom. Somebody spotted them and pointed. Others paused in their work to watch. At the bottom, Leacock stopped and screwed up his eyes, peering towards the heap of scrap. Meg watched him anxiously.

'Is there – anything, sir?'

The teacher shook his head. 'Nothing I can identify, but I suppose since we've come this far I might as well have a look at what's still in the swamp.' He set off across the soggy ground and Meg followed, dodging puddles. A few of the workers stood watching them from the pathway.

When they were still some yards off, Leacock called out, 'Where's your foreman?'

'Why?' shouted some wag in reply. 'Looking for work are you?' His companions laughed, but as the pair reached the pathway a stubby man in green dungarees stepped forward. Meg recognised him as Tracey Sugden's father.

'I'm foreman,' he growled. 'What's up?'

'I'd – like you to stop work for a few minutes,' Leacock told him. 'I have reason to believe there's a wartime bomber in that marsh and there could be bombs on board.' He said it as though he didn't believe it himself, and Meg doubted that it would impress Sugden. It didn't.

'You what?' he sneered. 'You must think I've just hatched out or summat. You're one o' them nuts that's been marching and protesting all over the place, aren't you?'

'No, I'm not!' snapped Leacock. 'I'm entirely in favour of this scheme, but it's possible your men are in great danger. I'm an authority on wartime aircraft in a small way, and if you'll just ask them to stop working for a few minutes I'd like to go in there and have a look at the metal objects you're finding.'

'Aye, I dare say.' The foreman stared hard at Meg. 'I know you, don't I?' he said. 'You're a Raven, aren't you? Your brother said summat to me about a plane this morning. I told 'im to fozz off. And your grandad runs that so-called Preservation Society.' He turned to the group of boys and men.

'You've not seen any bombers kicking about, have you lads?'

They grinned and shook their heads. One said, 'Me and

Eddie found one, only Stan said it was his, so we give it him back.' The others laughed.

The foreman looked at Leacock. 'There y'are,' he said. 'So you can go back and tell your mates you didn't manage to stop the job – tell 'em they'll need to come up with summat better than that to fool Ted Sugden.'

'Look!' cried the teacher. 'I told you – I have no connection with that damned Preservation Society. I . . .'

He broke off as the sound of chanting reached them. Everybody turned. Up on the footpath a procession appeared, waving placards. Two motorbikes wove in and out among the protestors. When it reached a point directly above them, the procession stopped and the demonstrators stood, looking down and chanting,

> 'Judy Woods is here to stay –
> Townhall vandals go away!'

Some of the workmen shouted back at them, waving shovels. Sugden turned to Leacock with a triumphant leer.

'So you've no connection wi' that lot, eh? Funny how they just happen to show up two minutes behind you then, innit?'

Meg whirled on him, shaking. 'There is a plane!' she shrieked. 'I know there is.'

'It's no use, Meg,' said Leacock resignedly. 'Not now.'

'No,' growled Sugden, 'nor never was neither. I'd make myself scarce if I was you, before these lads decide to duff you up.'

Meg could hear the earth-mover chugging in the Hollow. 'Stop him!' she screamed, and darted forward.

Sugden side-stepped and grabbed her by the arm. 'No you don't!' he grunted, and half-threw the struggling girl towards Leacock. The teacher caught her and began steering her away.

'Come along, Meg,' he urged. 'There's probably nothing here, you know. It was a nightmare, that's all.'

'No!' With a prodigious wrench she tore herself from his grip, leapt off the pathway and ran for the slope. 'Grandad!' she yelled, squinting through her tears at the crowd on the footpath above. 'Grandad!' She began to scramble up the bank. The figure of Henry Boyle detached itself and started down to meet her.

When she was just below him she gasped, 'A bomb – get Paul, Grandad, quick!' The old man hesitated.

'Bomb? What the heck you on about, Meg?' She came level with him.

'There's a plane in the Hollow with a bomb in it,' she choked. 'They won't believe me and Paul's right on top of it.'

'Plane?' Boyle's tone was one of incredulity. 'There's no plane in Boggy Hollow, lass!'

'There is, though,' growled a voice from the footpath.

The old man turned his head sharply. 'What d'you say, Dan Stamper?'

The farmer looked at his feet and mumbled, 'There is a plane. Came down in forty-three. Killed nine o' my flippin' pigs.'

'What – and you never . . .?' He turned to Meg. 'All right lass,' he rapped. 'Take me to where your brother is, and look sharp about it!'

Meg whirled and went bounding down the slope with the old man at her heels. The protestors flung aside their placards and followed their leader, pouring over the lip of the bank like lemmings over a cliff.

When Meg reached the pathway, Leacock yelled, 'What's happening?'

'There is a plane!' flung back Meg, as she pelted by with her grandad in hot pursuit.

'Good grief!' The teacher stared after them for a moment, then ran back towards the bank, dodging through the swarm of protestors who were charging towards the pathway.

Sugden, on the point of ordering Meg and the old man seized, saw the approaching mob and changed his mind. He stood by the road-roller, watching helplessly and muttering 'Hooligans' to himself as the horde swept by.

Meg and old Henry ran down into the Hollow. Trees crowded up to the pathway on either side, the nearest ones smashed to pale splinters. They ran on. Ahead, some thin, muddy alders lay scattered on the path. Four boys in dungarees and wellingtons were dragging these to one side and stacking them. They looked up as the two runners approached. A few yards beyond them the pathway petered out and there, on the very newest bit of it stood the earth-mover in a haze of blue exhaust. The great bucket swung at the end of its boom, out over the marsh, smashing down trees which it later would scoop from the mud. Directly below the clanking bucket, half-buried under fallen trees, something was sticking up out of the ooze: something big and buckled and metallic that might have been almost anything, but a glimpse of which made Meg's blood run cold.

'Paul!' She tried to shout but she was exhausted and the croak she uttered was drowned by the engine noise.

'Stay back, Meg!' Her grandfather brushed past her, scattered the knot of startled boys and hammered with his fists on the side of the vehicle's cab. In the cabin, Paul glanced sideways and was amazed to see old Henry's face gurning up at him from knee-level. He twisted round in his seat to see what was going on behind and there was Meg, moving her mouth and waving her arms at his workmates. He glanced beyond them and saw protestors pouring like a tidal wave along the pathway he had laid. He groaned.

Henry was banging on the cab again. Paul stuck his head out. 'Go away, Grandad!' he yelled. 'Don't you people know when you're licked?' He revved the engine, juggled the controls and skittled another batch of trees.

Meg was shouting at the four boys, pleading with them to abandon their work and run but, as the main body of protestors came in sight, their expressions hardened.

'Plane, my foot!' sneered one.

'Aye, and bomb my other foot and all,' added another. 'You're part of this mob, aren't you – trying it on?'

Meanwhile, Leacock was gasping out instructions to the bike-boys up on the footpath. 'Ride to the nearest phone,' he panted. 'Dial nine nine nine. Get all three emergency services out here. All three, right? Tell 'em it's a bomb.'

One boy shook his head. 'Not me, mate. They'd never believe me. I'm on bail for wrecking this joint.' He turned to his companion. 'You go, Les.'

'Right:' The lad flipped down his visor, twisted his throttle and roared away. The other boy got off his bike and lifted it on to its stand.

'What are you going to do?' asked Leacock.

'Me?' said Radar. 'I'm off down there of course.'

The earth-mover roared, lurched and started to back up. Old Henry leapt clear. Paul crouched over his controls, looking straight ahead. The boom dipped. The bucket hit the mud. Paul threw the machine into gear and it rolled forward, ramming the bucket under the fallen trees. As the boom came up, the bucket struck the half-submerged mass of metal. There was a clang and a grinding screech. The load tilted, slid and fell back into the mud.

Paul, mouthing furiously, grabbed the gear-lever and threw the vehicle so violently into reverse that a shower of chippings flew from under its wheels. Seeing what the boy meant to do, Henry Boyle dashed forward and tried to haul himself up to the cab. The machine jerked to a halt and he clung there with his boots off the ground and his mouth pressed against the dirty glass, shouting.

'Paul! Don't hit that thing again – there's a bomb!' The lad didn't even glance sideways. He dropped the boom, aimed the bucket at the obstruction and slammed the machine into gear. It rolled forward, gathering momentum. The old man clung on as the vehicle bounced and lurched over the uneven track. A few second more and the bucket would strike the plane. He bellowed and banged his head against the window but it was useless. He screwed up his eyes, waiting for the impact.

The bucket was six feet from its mark when the driver threw up his arms and the earth-mover slewed violently to the right. Its offside wheel hit the very edge of the track and skidded off in a hail of chippings. Sheer weight drove the wheel deep into the mud and the vehicle keeled over and came to rest on its side with Henry underneath.

On the pathway all was confusion. Workers and protestors milled about, shouting and shoving. Leacock, on top of the tree-pile, tried to make himself heard. Meg screamed, pointing to the earth-mover. A red-helmeted figure broke away and ran towards it. As he approached it a door lifted. Paul hauled himself out of the cab, staggered across the side of the machine and half-fell on to the pathway. Meg ran to him.

Radar plunged into the marsh and waded round the stricken vehicle as fast as the mud would allow, until he came to Henry Boyle. Only the top of the old fellow's head was visible. Kneeling, the lad plunged his hands into the ooze and locked them under Henry's chin. He swayed back, and the face broke the surface. Bending forward, he supported the head on one arm and with his free hand, clawed the stinking mud from nose and mouth before clamping his own mouth over Henry's in the kiss of life.

On the woodpile, Leacock had finally got everybody's attention. 'That object,' he shouted, pointing to the hump of blackened metal, 'is a Lancaster bomber of World War Two, and there may be bombs on board. If there are, they'll be in a highly dangerous condition. They've been disturbed, and could explode at any time. Emergency services are on their way, and I want everyone to leave the area immediately.' He found Sugden in the sea of faces and treated him to a baleful stare, adding, 'This is not a stunt.'

He climbed down, mopping his brow. The crowd was dispersing quite rapidly. Only Meg and Paul weren't moving. They stood, watching the hunched figure of Radar, half-visible beyond the sinking earth-mover.

'Come on, you two,' he said. 'There's nothing you can do here.'

Meg nodded towards Radar. 'What about them, sir?'

'I'll take over from the boy,' he said. 'Till the emergency services get here.' He called out to Radar, 'How is the old man, lad?'

The helmet appeared. 'Breathing, but I can't shift him. He's pinned under the machine.'

'Right. Hold on a sec and I'll take over.'

Radar straightened up and looked at him across the vehicle. 'Get lost. I'm not leaving the old guy now.'

Leacock pointed to the plane. 'Bombs, lad.'

Radar shrugged. 'So what're you – bomb-proof or summat?' He bent forward out of sight.

Leacock sighed and shook his head. 'Come on, you two.' The pathway was deserted. As they walked along it they could hear sirens in the distance.

Twenty-Nine

'Just my luck to have missed it all,' moaned Sally. It was the evening of the same day, and the two girls were sitting in the café.

'I know,' said Meg. 'That's why I thought we'd meet here, so I could tell you all about it.' She spoke quietly, because there were other customers in the café.

'It's not the same.'

'I know it's not, silly. Anyway, I was saying about Desperate Dan. Grandad was just about to tell me I was talking rubbish or something, when he chipped in and said yes, there was a plane in Boggy Hollow because it had killed nine of his pigs. I don't get that – what would pigs be doing in Boggy Hollow?'

Mabel, wiping a nearby table and eavesdropping said, 'I can answer that, love.' She came over and lowered her voice.

'In the war, meat was rationed. Farmers had to tell the government how many pigs they had, so that when the pigs were killed the meat could be shared out fairly. But Dan Stamper was a cheat. If one of his sows had ten piglets, he'd tell the government it'd had eight. He'd hide the other two in a secret sty in Boggy Hollow. He'd do that with all his sows, and then when the secret piglets were all fattened up, he'd smuggle 'em out at night and sell them for a lot of money.'

Meg frowned. 'And that's why he never told about the bomber?'

Mabel nodded. 'If he'd told, there'd have been people all over his farm – officials and that. They'd have found his secret sty and he'd have gone to prison.'

'But what an awful thing to do!' cried Sally. 'Letting those poor airmen lie there all that time and nobody knowing what happened to them. Will they put him in prison now?'

Mabel shrugged. 'I don't know, love. It was all a long time

ago. I expect he'll move away though – he won't dare show his face round here any more.'

'What I want to know,' whispered Meg, when Mabel had moved away, 'is who the airmen were.'

'Why?'

'Because I think I know already, Sal.'

'Don't be daft. How could you?'

'Remember those ghosts I saw?'

Sally laughed. 'Those ghosts you said you saw, yes. What about them?'

'They were the airmen.'

'Were they heck!'

'Yes, they were. How d'you think I knew about the plane?'

Sally shrugged. 'I don't know, but I don't believe all that stuff about ghosts. There's no such thing as ghosts – my dad told me.'

'Then your dad's wrong for once. You wait till they release the names – I bet you one's called Lockyer and one's called Lee and one's called Hanlon. He was my grandad – my real one.'

Sally smiled and shook her head. 'You're crazy, Meg. I'd bet you a pound if I had one.'

Meg was about to suggest that Sally bet her new video game instead, when the door opened and Paul walked in. 'Hi, you two!' He passed them and went over to the counter.

'Hi yourself,' muttered Meg. 'D'you know, Sal – that pig didn't believe us? Even with grandad hanging on the outside of his precious earth-mover he didn't believe us. He's as bad as you and Mum.'

Paul came over with three cokes and sat down. 'Here – I got you drinks.' He slid cans in front of the girls and took a long pull from his own. Meg looked at him.

'Won the pools, have you?'

He grinned. 'Don't be like that. I've got good news for you.'

His sister eyed him narrowly. 'What news?'

'Two bits, actually. The first is, your bike-boy hero's off the hook.'

'Radar?' Meg frowned. 'How d'you mean, off the hook?'

'The vandalism thing. He didn't do it. Dan Stamper did.'

'Dan Stamper?' Sally gaped. 'But it said York aggro on the wall.'

Paul nodded. 'He did that so the bike-boys'd get the blame, but when he heard how your friend Radar wouldn't leave old Henry this morning, he owned up. They found four five-hundred pound bombs in the plane, by the way – all rotten and ready to blow.'

'Ugh!' Meg shivered. 'What's the other bit of news?'

'Mum and Dad just got back from the hospital. Henry's got shock and some cracked ribs, but the doctors say he's going to be all right. They're amazed, because he's got a dodgy heart and he was belting about like a two-year-old this morning.'

'It's a good job for us that he was,' said Meg. 'He saved our lives y'know. If he hadn't made you swerve you'd have hit that wreckage and we'd all have been blown to kingdom come.'

Paul shook his head. 'Old Henry didn't make me swerve. It was those daft protestors in fancy dress.'

Meg frowned. 'None of the protestors was anywhere near you,' she said. 'They were all behind.'

'Not all,' the boy contradicted. 'Seven of 'em appeared out of nowhere and plonked themselves smack in front of me. I was nearly on top of 'em and they just stood there in a line, grinning. If I hadn't swerved they'd have died whether the bombs went off or not.'

Meg was silent for a moment. Then she smiled sadly, knowing she would not be believed. 'No, Paul,' she murmured. 'They wouldn't. You see – they were dead already.'

Thirty

Next day, some men from the Ministry of Defence came and poked about in Boggy Hollow. The remains of seven men were removed from the bomber and identified by their dog-tags, and it was just as Meg had said.

They were buried two days later in the churchyard, where the guard of honour fired a volley that set the jackdaws wheeling round the tower. A handful of strangers were there – relatives of the other men. Some had come quite a long way. Meg's grandmother cried a bit, then took them all back to Fox Place for tea.

Mrs Raven went about for a couple of days looking thoughtful. Then she tore up the book she'd been writing, shut herself in her room and started again.

When the men from the Ministry had gone, Leacock and some of his friends dug out the decaying Lancaster and carted it off, piece by piece, to the museum they ran on the site of a disused railway station, and began to re-assemble it. It would eventually be displayed, with photographs and details of its career as a memorial to its crew.

As Paul had predicted, all charges against Radar were dropped. When he heard the news, the lad rode out to Stamper's farm with the idea of thanking the old villain for clearing his name. He found the place deserted, and that evening he returned with his friends. The property was so dilapidated and overgrown as to be almost useless as a farm, but parts of it would make an ideal scramble-track. 'When one door closes,' he grinned, 'another opens.'

Once the business in Boggy Hollow was over, the project proceeded smoothly. With its leader in hospital and the site so obviously improved, the Judy Woods Preservation Society faded quietly away, and by the end of June the job was finished.

The twenty-first of July was set aside for the official opening, and a well-known T.V. personality was to perform the ceremony.

The day dawned bright and clear and the whole village, together with many sightseers from York, trooped along the concrete path across the field. The new fence had a ticket-box in its gateway, and a green tape had been stretched across the entrance for the T.V. personality to cut. A brass band played near the gateway and beyond it Len and Mabel stood smiling, as well they might, in the doorway of the café.

Meg and Sally arrived early and bagged themselves places near the tape. They were soon glad they had, because by a quarter-to eleven the place was packed. At five-to there was a buzz of excitement in the crowd as a white Rolls-Royce appeared. It cruised silently up to the gateway and the personality got out. He wore a black leather jacket and dark glasses and was smaller than Meg had expected. He glanced about him.

'This is the queue for the gents, isn't it?' Everybody laughed, and he did a quick shuffle and flashed his teeth at them.

'It's all right you lot laughing,' he went on. 'You didn't stop at my hotel last night. Filthy, that hotel – filthy!' Sniggers in the crowd. 'In fact it was so filthy they put a pig in my room as an air-freshener.' There was a roar of laughter and some clapping. The personality grinned shyly and held up his hands, as if he hadn't expected applause and was embarrassed.

'What a poser!' whispered Sally, but Meg, drowsy with the sun's warmth and happier than she could remember, smiled and murmured, 'He's all right.'

After a couple of speeches the tape was cut, the band struck up a rousing march and the crowd began streaming through into the nature park and leisure reserve, while the T.V. personality leant against the bonnet of the Rolls-Royce, signing autographs.

Meg and Sally were among the first through. They made a bee-line for the café, bought cokes and grabbed a table by the window. Others poured in and soon the place was full. Chairlegs screeched. People chattered. The cash-register whirred. Len and Mabel beamed.

Meg sat with her elbows on the table and her chin in her

hands, watching the scene outside. Small children swarmed over the playground and clung in heaving clusters to the rides. Men and women in bright summer clothes moved to and fro, greeting friends and pointing things out to one-another in the dappled sunlight. Sally frowned at the back of her friend's head.

'Hey,' she said. 'You're with me, remember?'

'What?' Meg turned. 'Oh, sorry, Sal. I was thinking.'

'Dreaming, more like.' She toyed with her coke-tin. 'You've been miles away all morning, Meg – what you thinking about?'

'Oh.' Meg shrugged. 'Nothing much. Just how nice it is to be able to call your grandad Grandad without your mother jumping down your throat.'

'Huh?' Sally scowled. 'You're crazy, Meg Raven.'

Meg shook her head. 'No, Sal – I'm not, and that's another thing that's nice.' Sally puzzled for a moment and then her face cleared. 'No more ghosts?'

Meg smiled. How restful at last to be understood. 'No more ghosts,' she said.